Cosmic

Whispers

Lorin C Saunders

Illustrations

L. B. Lee

Books
Publishing LLC

Books Publishing LLC
11801 W. Executive Drive
Boise, ID 83713.
E-mail: lcs@bookspublishing.net
www.bookspublishing.net

Printed in the United States of America
First Printing: January 1999.

Library of Congress Cataloging-in-Publication Data

Saunders, Lorin C, 1930—
Cosmic Whispers: Philosophical poetry dealing with the
visual and inner evidence in favor of life's continuum as
opposed to atheistic evolution.

Includes research notes and comments, and twenty
illustrations by L .B. Lee.

Library of Congress Catalog Card Number: 98-92290

ISBN: 0-9669208-0-5

This book is dedicated to
Cleo,
my wife and best friend.

Table of Contents

PART ONE

EVIDENTIAL THOUGHTS

PART TWO

THOUGHTS TO CONSIDER

Sketches

Acknowledgments

In preparing *Cosmic Whispers* for publication, I had the good fortune of being assisted by Joy Saunders Lundberg, Gary Lundberg, Diane Elsworth, Lee R. Saunders, and Dr. William C. Overton of Boise State University. My sister Joy's encouragement and her approval of my work has given me the courage to publish this book.

I would also like to thank my wife, Cleo, and Shirleen Meek Saunders for their invaluable contributions.

Preface

At the time of the publication of Charles Darwin's *The Origin of Species*, in 1859, science had been moving away from accepting any supernatural interventions in the physical sciences. Science was taking the position that rational thought cannot consider seriously matters beyond human experience or comprehension. Darwin, in the *Origin*, was extending natural phenomenon to the biological sciences.[1]

Darwin's "theory of evolution" introduced an idea that materialistic thought could understand. It defined biological creation as a product of chance mutation from the simplest cells to its present state of variety and complexity, thereby eliminating the need for a Creator.

Atheism and Darwinian evolution are natural companions. (The terms are used synonymously throughout *Cosmic Whispers*.) Darwin's theory gave new life and meaning to this age-old philosophical delusion. His theory "broke man's link with his creator and set him adrift in a cosmos without purpose"[2] —nothing more than a rare accident in time.

The scientific community found Darwin's ideas so rational that within a few years after his theory was published, it became an irrefutable axiom of science. Since then nearly all acceptable scientific research on man's origin has been done to verify, not disprove, Darwin's theory. Thenceforth, evolution has been the "light which illuminates all facts."[3] In academe, other alternative views are not considered worthy of intellectual thought. According to science, its own rules of observation and objective research need not be further applied to the basic assumptions of this theory.

To science, evolution's destiny is secure as an impregnable paradigm of fact. [3]

Few ideas have permeated society as has Darwin's theory of evolution. Still, it is only a theory, which, according to many scholars, is without a shred of empirical evidence.

Darwin's "theory of evolution" has been identified as a major cause in the decline of moral values in the western world. Its philosophy is far-reaching and, though at conflict with the faith and thinking of the majority of humanity, its tentacles reach out to strangle the moral breath of society. When it is accepted that hope and belief in immortality are nothing more than "sentimental nonsense" and that "above man there is no supreme being," but instead that man is "the crowning glory of the universe" and that meeting his needs and desires are the "supreme imperatives" of existence, then the moral fabric of society begins to unravel. [4]

To nourish a belief of immortal hopelessness betrays the reality of eternal consequence and accountability, and opens the gates of selfish indulgence and carnal sensuality. Noble thoughts of duty, loyalty, and sacrifice flee like chaff before the winds of desire and are replaced by hedonistic whims to be satisfied before annihilation begins.

> What matter the course we run
> Or the deeds we've done,
> If all is forgotten in oblivion.

Still, today, in spite of this moral dilemma, the philosophies of atheism and evolution are firmly seated in academic studies, even at the earliest levels of education. Though there are well-documented, scholarly arguments that identify evolution's weaknesses, uncertainties, and missing links, they are not allowed in the sacred halls of academe. To not juxtapose these arguments with the theory of evolution is an affront to the search for truth. [5]

Darwin himself acknowledged problems with his theory. He said that it was in jeopardy if the fossil record failed to provide considerable transitional evidence of mutation of species. In his day there was an absence of such evidence, but he hoped time would validate his ideas.[6]

After over a century of searching, the fossil record still remains silent when it comes to transitional forms of life. There is, however, resounding evidence of stasis, which is the antithesis of Darwinian evolution. All that seems necessary to explain away these inconsistencies and missing links, according to science, is a few million or billion years.[7]

Time, according to science, is on the side of evolution. Yet according to mathematical improbabilities, there is simply not enough time for such specificity to emerge by chance in a universe estimated by science to be only 10^{18} seconds old. If mutation were possible, nature and earth could never mutate in their time frame the variety of life they claim.

For instance, consider the immense number of possible permutations of the 574 amino-acid positions that make up the molecule hemoglobin. They are so specific in their organization that if these amino acids had been shuffled every second for the life of the universe, they could never have come together by chance in the precise order required to form hemoglobin. Hemoglobin has an improbability of chance organization approaching 10^{650}. And if we consider DNA, with its voluminous script of chemical memory equaling 10,000 miles of computer printout, we begin to understand the impossible odds of any meaningful chance formulation in a universe estimated by science to be only 10^{18} seconds old. When we look at these cosmic numbers the meaning of the word *never* begins to emerge.

Darwin totally underestimated the time his theory would need: trillions of times longer than the existence of the universe. Even then it would be impossible for blind chance to work such a miracle. [8]

Little wonder, when presented with the reality of these odds, that Julian Huxley, a descendant of the distinguished biologist Thomas Huxley, a protagonist of Darwin's theory of evolution, declared, "But if it is not natural selection working on random variation, what can it be? What can it be?" [9]

And then there is life itself. Science acknowledges that it has never been able to open the secrets of life's being. Between the elements and their animation with life lies an unbreachable chasm beyond the reach of human ingenuity, a chasm that elements alone cannot cross. [10]

The discoveries in molecular biology speak against chance mutation. Even if chance could accidentally organize something meaningful, it could never, in all eternity, organize the beauty and complexity of the biological world.

The elegance and perfection in molecular biology are the antitheses of chance. Living organisms consist of numerous, complex parts that have to work together to sustain life, which compounds their purpose and specificity and further precludes chance. We can trace the majesty of biological life to its beginnings, from its cells to its molecules, atoms, and electrons. We can identify the directing force of the DNA molecule and the majesty of its code or program, but beyond this point we must search for the Programer. [11]

The visible reality of another dimension of invisible, yet real, existence manifests itself in the biological world and is personified in life. How science can work among such microscopic perfections, specificity, and complexity and not develop a reverence for a further reality beyond the visible is incomprehensible.

The theory of evolution should provide nothing more than one of the platforms from which to launch discussions on the origin of life, not a platform from which all other ideas are dusted away as insignificant. "The knowledge that we are here, so we must have evolved somehow," remains an impenetrable paradigm of science. The possibility of a Creator is never allowed to enter the equation.

Science requires empirical evidence from all opposing philosophical views while it glories in speculative theory. When it comes to the scientific explanations of evolution, we hear statements such as "given enough time," "we must assume," "appears to have happened," "it is conceivable," "we may infer". It is difficult to understand how rational conviction can be born of such ambiguity.

Much of the poetry in *Cosmic Whispers* deals with the inner, visual, and rational evidences that speak their veritable sounds in favor of a reality beyond the visible world and universe. To the perceptive, the cosmos whispers convincing evidence of this reality.

Cosmic Whispers also speaks to reason and rational argument against the greatest fraud ever perpetrated on humanity. But more than being against evolution and atheism they are thoughts in reverence of the visual and inner evidences that inspire respect for the Creator of the glory that surrounds us. They are my private thoughts and feelings, but I take great comfort in believing that most of them echo in the hearts of the vast majority of humanity, and that they have supportive value that can help us through the maze of atheistic sophistry besieging us today.

Lorin C Saunders

Part One

Evidential

Thoughts

Atheism's Flight

ATHEISM DESCENDS UPON A LONELY FLIGHT
INTO A DARK AND OBLIVIOUS NIGHT.

DRIVEN BY AN ACADEMIC FEW—
THE UNIVERSITIES, SCHOOLS,
TEXTBOOKS, AND PERIODICALS—
ALL SPEAK THEIR POSTULATIONS AS TRUTHS;
DECEIVING THE INNOCENT, SUSCEPTIBLE MIND
WITH THEIR PHILOSOPHICAL, MALIGNANT FINDS.

ATHEISM'S BETRAYAL OF HOPE,
OF BINDING TIES,
OF CONTINUING LIVES,
BELIES ETERNAL VERITIES.

AND THOSE WHO VENTURE ITS CAVERNOUS ABYSS
SOON DISCOVER ITS FRAUDULENT DISGUISE
WHEN ETERNITY OPENS THEIR EYES.

1

Atoms of Immortality

WHEN WHAT OTHERWISE IS STILL AND LIFELESS
FUSES WITH THE RIBBONS
OF IMMORTAL HEREDITY,
WE GLIMPSE THE UNSEEABLE
AND ENDLESS PATTERNS OF INNUMERABLE GENES.

THE REFINED ELEMENTS OF THE INVISIBLE WORLD
PERSONIFY BEFORE US
IN BIOLOGICAL FORMULATIONS.

WITHIN THE MOLECULES OF LIFE
WE TOUCH AN ENDLESS DESTINY.

"Be Fruitful and Multiply"

"BE FRUITFUL AND MULTIPLY"
WAS THE COMMAND ON EARTH.

SO GLORIOUS AND WONDERFUL
IS NATURE'S BIRTH—

SO PURPOSEFUL IN ATTRACTION,
SO BEAUTIFUL IN FORM,
SO WONDROUS IN EMOTION,
SO RESPONSIBLE A DEVOTION,
SO SPECIFICALLY DESIGNED—
MALE AND FEMALE COMBINED
TO BRING FORTH THEIR KIND.

PURPOSE IS EVERYWHERE DEFINED.

Chance

It is impossible to create beauty and genius by chance.

The beauty, variety, and unimaginable glory
Of life on earth
Defies evolutionary logic
And revels against chance's fated course
Toward disorder and confusion.

Chance's unpredictable destiny
Holds only lifeless, inert matter
Within its entropic [13] spell,
And human stupor is exponentially magnified
In science and philosophy's
Nihilistic rampages.

Child

Whoever looks upon a child sees immortality face to face.

I LOOKED UPON MY CHILD'S EAR
AND BEHELD THE CURVATURES SO FINE.

I LOOKED UPON THE BEAUTY
OF HER REST COMBINED.

WHENCE COMETH THIS CHILD OF MINE?
WHENCE, HER WONDROUS MIND?

I LOOKED UPON MY CHILD'S FACE
AND PEERED INTO HER EYES
AND SAW, WITH INSTANT FAITH,
BEYOND HER MORTAL DISGUISE.

Clock

As we examine the clock's
Mechanical wonder
And its exactness
As it points time's numbers,

It becomes evident
That the clock could never,
In all cosmic time,
Answer chance's paradigm.

It must be
A product of design.

So the vastly more-complicated
Human form
Could never
By chance be born.

Each carries the stamp
Of its creator's hand.
Each as evidence
Doth indisputably stand. [14]

Contemplation

As I come quietly to the time
When my course is nearly run—

As I ponder upon my past
And review all I've done—

When I consider my friends, loved ones,
And all those I've known before
Who have silently closed their door—
The great minds,
The poets, musicians, scientists,
And their kind,
And the simple folk like me—

When I consider the beauties of nature,
The flowers and trees,
The mountain lakes and spacious seas,
And the majesty out there
Beyond earth's atmosphere—

I have to believe there is more to life
Than I can see.

The order and wonder of nature and space,
And the human race,
Could not be a waste.

Cosmic Beings

Our individuality extends far beyond mortality.

WITHIN OUR BODIES COURSE
THE ELEMENTS OF THE COSMOS.

THE ELEMENTS THAT FLAME THE SUN,
THE STARS, AND THE GALAXIES ARE OURS.
THEY COME ALIVE IN LIVING BEINGS AND THINGS
TO GROW, BREATHE,
BLOSSOM, REASON, AND DREAM.

STILL, THE DEEPER KNOWLEDGE
OF COSMIC FORMULATIONS,
THAT ORGANIZE AND ANIMATE,
REMAIN RESTRAINED IN THEIR LOFTY TOWERS.

SO SPECIFIC IN THEIR ORDER
THAT ONLY FOOLISH CONJECTURE,
GUESSES, AND KNOWLEDGE TURNED SOUR
CAN SEPARATE THEIR SPECIFICITY [15] AND PURPOSE
FROM THE ETERNAL SOURCE
OF THEIR DIRECTING POWER.

THOUGH HIDDEN FROM MORTAL VIEW
THEIR VARIETY OF LIFE IS HERE, ONLY RENEWED.

The unseen images
And patterns of the cosmos
Continue reflecting their kind
As they propagate
And replenish in earthen time.

Soon, unrestrained by mortal limitations,
Cosmic cathedral doors
Will open wide their infinite stores.

What sudden enlightenment
To agnostic thought—
To immortal beings,
As their eternal nature
Upon the future beams.

Cosmic Whispers

If we are sensitive to the echoes
Of the cosmos, and listen—
They speak their empirical confirmations
Of our imperishable identity and purpose
In the sidereal foreverness.

In every view of nature and celestial glory
The cosmos whispers its immortal sounds.

You hear them deep within conscious thought
As reason mingles with its peers,
Drawing the endless theophany ever near.

You hear its continuous pleading
As you listen—
As it speaks
To wrest the dormant faith of humanity
From its slumber.

Creation's Witness

HIGH IN EARTHLY SKIES WE FLY
IN GIANT MECHANICAL BIRDS,
SYMBOLS OF OUR DOMINION,
AS THEIR MIGHTY ROARS ARE HEARD.

WE RIDE THE EXPRESSES UPWARD
IN CONCRETE TOWERS
AND MARVEL AT OUR CREATIVE POWERS.

WE SEE OUR MASTERY OVER ELEMENTS OF EARTH:
GOLD, SILVER, IRON, AND MINERALS OF WORTH.

EVEN WITH THE MOLECULES OF LIFE
OUR EXPRESSIVE POWER IS RIFE.

EACH OF OUR CREATIONS
EVIDENCE PURPOSE AND DESIGN,
EACH THE WORK OF MYSTERIOUSLY WONDROUS MINDS,
EACH EVIDENCE GENIUS
EVOLUTIONARY CHANCE COULD NEVER FIND.

Deistic Thought

When atheistic philosophers
Retire in reminiscence
And wrestle
With their secret thoughts;

When their fatalistic gaze
Rests upon the complexities
And beauty of nature
And biological wonder;

Or view the elegance of human beings
With their thoughts, works of art,
Vocal expressions, and genius;

They must have moments where doubt
Ripples among their philosophical thoughts
Catching glimpses of immortal hope.

Delusion

To nourish a belief of immortal hopelessness,
Atheism, or evolution
Betrays the reality of
Eternal consequence and accountability
And opens the gates
Of selfish indulgence and carnal sensuality.

Noble thoughts of duty, loyalty, and sacrifice
Flee, like chaff, before the winds of desire,
Replaced by hedonistic whims,
To be satisfied before annihilation begins.

What matter the course we run,
Or the deeds we've done,
If all is forgotten in oblivion?

What horror when eternal light
Lays its rays upon us,
And those embraced in delusion's grasp
See their acts before them pass!

Make no mistake, fellow travelers,
All actions are recorded in cosmic past
To serve our memory lapse.

Earth's Glory

THE EARTH IS ADORNED WITH BEAUTY,
SYMMETRY, AND GRACEFUL LINES
THAT PERSONIFY PLANNING, PURPOSE, AND DESIGN.

FROM THE ROLLING CLOUDS IN BROKEN BLUE SKIES
TO THE GOLDEN FINDS OF A RAINBOW'S PRIZE—

FROM THE OCEAN DEPTHS AND WAVES THAT RISE
AS THE MOON GLIDES
THROUGH THE MIDNIGHT SKIES—

TO THE MORNING SUN
AS IT AWAKENS ACROSS EASTERN DAWN
WITH WARMTH, WONDER, LIGHT, AND SONG,
THEN SETS AS EVENING COMES,
NUDGING THE MOON AGAIN TO RUN—

SO BEAUTIFUL AND RESPLENDENT TO BEHOLD
IS OUR WONDROUS EARTHLY GLOBE
AS IT ROLLS IN GLORY WITH ITS CELESTIAL KIN,
REFLECTING ELSEWHERE PATTERNS WITHIN.

Echoes

OUT OF THE COSMIC THUNDER—
OUT OF THE MIDST OF WONDER—
COMES THE EARTH, THE MOON, AND THE SUN.

MAJESTICALLY THEY ROLL UPON THEIR WINGS.
HARMONIOUSLY THEIR PURPOSE RINGS
TO PROVIDE A HOME FOR LIVING THINGS.

OUT OF THE MOUNTAINS, VALLEYS, AND HILLS—
OUT OF THE FERTILE FIELDS—
BURSTS THE PROFUSION OF BOTANICAL BIRTH.

FROM IMMUTABLE SEEDS
THE EARTH COMES ALIVE
IN MELODIOUS SURPRISE.

THE SEASONS BEGIN
AS SPRING BREACHES THE FRIGID WINTER'S END
WITH ITS VIBRANT COLOR-BLENDS.

SOON SUMMER'S WARMTH IS FOUND,
THEN AUTUMN WITH ITS SHADES OF GOLDEN-BROWNS.
AGAIN WINTER COMES AROUND.

THE TROPICAL WONDER—
THE CLOUDS WITH THEIR MOISTURE AND THUNDER!

OUT OF THE PATTERNS OF THE PAST
WE REVIEW THEIR WONDROUS REPASS.

THE FLORA THAT COVERS THE EARTH,
THE INSECTS,
THE BIRDS,
THE NUMEROUS ANIMAL HERDS,
THE AQUATIC AND MARINE BEINGS—
IN ALL THAT LIFE BRINGS
CONSISTENCY ABOUNDS
WITH ECHOES OF STASIS SOUNDS.

PURPOSE SEEMS FUNDAMENTAL IN ALL THINGS
AS THE ANCESTRAL RECORD PROTECTS ITS GENES.

OUT OF THE COSMOS UNSEEN—
OUT OF IMMORTAL GENES—
IS BORN THE HUMAN FORM:
MAN AND WOMAN WITH IMMORTAL NORMS—
WITH HOPES, DREAMS, AND FOREVER THEMES.

NUMEROUS GIFTS UNFOLD,
EXPRESSING THE GENIUS
IN THE WONDROUS HUMAN SOUL
AS IT SPEAKS, REASONS, AND THINKS.

OUT OF THIS ORDERLY ARRAY—
OUT OF THIS PROFUSE DISPLAY—
CHANCE BOWS IN REVERENT DISMAY.

HARMONIOUSLY THIS THEOPHANIC SYMPHONY
ECHOES ITS CRESCENDO SOUNDS,
HERE, ONLY PARTIALLY PLAYED.

Like an unfinished love song
Searching for its final verse,
Or the early morning dawn
Longing for the sun's full burst,
This unfinished symphony
Waits for the call of the Maestro's baton
To continue its heraldic song.

Elements of Life

From the more pure elements
Of the universe—
Unseen, untouchable, untestable
By mortal senses—
Their substance so refined,
Still firmly defined—

Visible in their animation of nature—
The essence of self
That speaks, reasons, and thinks,
Where emotions are felt—
Everlasting in their being—
Comes life that forms nature and humankind.

Kindredly tangible,
We will come to know,
As forever their refinement flows—

Without their hold upon biological birth—
Unto dust the living earth!

This is the matter of the soul,
The substance of biological control.

Empirical Knowledge

Our very cry for empirical proof
Of the unseen world
Shines as evidence
Of immortality's presence.

The speaking, listening, learning,
Silent yearning
Resound their message
In thunderously quiet strains
That vibrate through every cry of hope,
Every image of thought,
Every conscious regret,
And emotion wrought—
Continually whispering
The reasoning impressions
Of the immortal soul.

They become our very touch
With inner reality,
The personification and tangible evidence
Of eternity,
That shines brightly every moment
Of our wakening hours,
And endlessly serves our empirical urge.

Eternal Similarities

I OFTEN WONDER
AS I PONDER UPON THE FUTURE—
WHAT WILL IT BE LIKE IN ETERNITY?

WHAT WILL THE FLOWERS AND NATURE BE?
AND THE BIRDS AND ANIMALS WE'LL SEE?

OUR FRIENDS AND THOSE WE'VE KNOWN BEFORE,
WHAT ARE THEY DOING AND LIVING FOR?

ARE THERE HOUSES, CONCERTS, WORK, AND PLAY,
AND FRIENDLY VISITS AT THE END OF DAY?

AS I LOOK AROUND AT THE GLORY OF NATURE
AND ITS BEAUTY HERE,
I WONDER, IS THIS LIFE A SHADOW OF THE PAST
AND FUTURE THAT ETERNITY CASTS?

ARE THE AWAKENINGS OF LIFE IN EARLY SPRING,
AND THE JOY THEY BRING,
A LIKENESS ETERNITY SINGS?

DOES ALL NATURE RHYME?
IS THIS THE ETERNITY I'LL FIND?

As I close my eyes to this mortal life
Could it be I'll find
Eternal harmony and familiarity
That will not be a surprise to me?
A place as real as my earthly home,
With sorrow, sickness, and evil unknown?

Where birds sing familiar songs?
Somewhere where nothing can go wrong?
Will this be the place where I'll belong?

I wonder!

Evolution's Fraud

I PONDER UPON A FLOWERING FIELD
AND THE VARIETY OF LIFE IT YIELDS;
THE SUN;
HOW NATURE IS FED;
THE CLOUDS WITH THEIR MOISTURE OVERHEAD;
THE HONEY BEE
WORKING FROM THE BLOSSOMS THE NECTAR FREE.

AS I EXAMINE MORE CLOSELY
NATURE'S BEAUTY, ELEGANCE, AND COMPLEXITY—
WHAT HARMONY AND MAJESTY I SEE!

HOW COULD ALL THIS BE
BY CHANCE MUTATIONS FROM AN ANCESTRAL SEA?

MEASURING THE TIME IT WOULD TAKE
FOR CHANCE TO CREATE, [12]
IS IMPOSSIBLE TO CALCULATE.

THE SIMPLEST FLOWER IN THE FIELD
IS SO COMPLEX IN ITS MOLECULAR BUILD,
IT WOULD TAKE MORE TIME THAN THE UNIVERSE
FOR A FLOWER TO BURST
AS A PRIMEVAL FIRST.

NOT THE MILLIONS OF YEARS ON EARTH
THAT SCIENCE CONTINUES TO REHEARSE,

While completely ignoring
The mathematical improbability.

As for me, a husbandman I see
Planting seeds in his nursery.

Which makes more sense
Than a primeval weed
From a mud-lake sea
After millions of years in slimy debris.

Don't you agree?

Hope

We may not see beyond mortal life
Or know for certain
What the future is like.

Still, there is an unexplained yearning—
A hope—quietly telling, churning.

The faith that inspires all progress on
Is the same that stirs eternal hope along.

We see it in the face of innocence,
In the feelings of a mother's sense,
And in older-ones' confidence.

It comes in the quietness of reminiscence
Where goodness and love combine,
Or, when wondering upon our future time.

It's then we come to trust
In hope's paradigm,
And leave uncertainty and doubt behind.

I Wonder

In my pensive, reminiscent dreams and hopes
I wonder upon the splendorous scenes—
Of the mystery cradled within their genes.

I feel the breeze weaving its way
Among the stately trees and forest glades,
The sun's dissipating rays
As it greets the morning mist
And warms the coming day.

I hear the ocean waves
And watch them sliding down the shores
Only to come again in thunderous roars.
I hear forever these sounds
And feel the warmth and beauty around—
And I wonder!

I see the birds riding the ocean crests,
Hear them singing in the trees,
See them building their nests—

I see and hear all of nature's wonders,
And I wonder!

I wander the quiet deserts
And rest on mountaintops
With only echoes and thoughts—
And wonder!

I HEAR THE THUNDER,
THE RAGING STORMS—THE LIVES THUS TORN—
AND I WONDER!

I HEAR THE CHILDREN'S LAUGHTER AND CRIES—
I SEE THE MYRIADS OF PEOPLE PASSING BY—
WITH THEIR TROUBLES, THOUGHTS, AND DREAMS—
AND I WONDER, WHY?

I VISIT THE STATELY CONCERT HALLS,
THE SANCTUARIES AND MUSEUMS;
I VIEW THE WONDROUS ART,
AND HEAR THE SOUNDS THEREIN.
I FEEL THE IMPRESSIONS AND BEAUTY
LEFT YEARS BEFORE MY KIN.
I FEEL THE PRESENCE
OF UNFORGOTTEN GENIUS WITHIN—
AND I WONDER!

I WATCH A ELDERLY WOMAN
CRADLE AN INFANT IN HER ARMS.
I SEE THE LENGTH OF MORTAL LIFE AND MORE
SILHOUETTED IN THESE FORMS.

THEIR EYES,
LOOKING INTO EACH OTHER'S,
FOREVER SEARCHING,
FOREVER REACHING
BEYOND THEIR MORTAL COVER—

AND WONDROUSLY, I WONDER!

I Write

I WRITE OF THE WIND, THE BREEZE,
THE RUSTLING LEAVES,
THE MOUNTAINS AND VALLEYS,
THE ROLLING HILLS AND MAJESTIC SEAS.

I WRITE OF THE TREES,
THE DESERT'S THIRST—ITS GOLDEN SUNSETS,
FLOWERS AND THE BEAUTY THAT COVER THE EARTH.

I WRITE OF THE BEES, OF THE BIRDS,
OF LIFE IN THE SEAS, AND OF GALLOPING HERDS.

I WRITE OF THE HUMAN FORM,
OF FOREVER NORMS,
THE GIFT OF REASON,
OF HUMANITY'S DIVINE IMAGE
AND ETERNAL MOORINGS.

I WRITE OF THE STARS, SUNS, AND GALAXIES;
THE MAJESTY OF SPACE;
OF THE IMMORTAL EVIDENCE LEFT TO TRACE.

I WRITE OF DESIGN AND PURPOSE,
OF THE WONDERS OF NATURE
AND THE GLORY OF THE HUMAN RACE.

Immortal Creation

DEEP WITHIN THE WOMAN DWELLS
CREATION'S BEGINNING CELLS.

LINKED IN FERTILE UNION,
WITHOUT CONSCIOUS DIRECTION ON HER PART,
THE RIBBONS OF HEREDITY—
WITH THEIR VOLUMINOUS SCRIPT
OF CHEMICAL MEMORY—
BEGIN TO UNFOLD,
SHAPE, AND MOLD
THE WONDROUS ART IN LIFE'S GENETIC CODE.

CELLS BECOME DEPENDENT
AS THEY MULTIPLY IN THEIR COMPLEXITY,
FORM BONDS, CONVERSE,
SCHEDULE, AND REFLECT.

CONTINUALLY WHISPERING
THEIR CHEMICAL DIRECTIONS,
THEY BEGIN THEIR MYSTERIOUS JOURNEY
TOWARD HUMAN PERFECTION.

SOON, UNPRECEDENTED DETAILS BECOME CLEAR.
GREAT BEAUTY, ARTISTRY,
AND WONDROUS SHAPES APPEAR.

As CELLS MULTIPLY AND BOND
THEY FORM INTIMATE RELATIONSHIPS
THAT COMPOSE THE COMPLEX UNIVERSE
OF THE BODY AND SOUL.

A SPINAL CORD AND NERVOUS SYSTEM DEVELOPS.
A BONE STRUCTURE
WITH MUSCLES AND TENDONS ENVELOP.

THE HEART, LUNGS, KIDNEYS, AND GLANDS BEGIN;
IMAGES AND REFLECTIONS OF FORMER KIN,
AS COMES THE COVERING OF SKIN.

THE MARVEL OF THE HUMAN EAR
IS SOON TO HEAR ALL LIFE'S REFRAINS,
INTERPRETED, SORTED, AND RETAINED
IN THE CONVOLUTIONS
OF THE MYSTERIOUSLY DEVELOPING BRAIN.

WITH LENS AND RETINA, RODS AND CONES,
THE HUMAN EYES PERFECTION MOLDS.
WHERE MILLIONS OF CELLS MULTIPLY,
EACH IN PERFECTION ON THE OTHERS RELIES
TO TRANSFORM LIGHT INTO GLORIOUS SIGHT.

THE SENSES OF TASTE AND SMELL
DEVELOP, AS WELL;
AND WARMTH AND COLD, AS THE SENSES UNFOLD
TO HOLD MEMORIES THROUGHOUT YEARS:

A walk through the park—
The shuffling, rustling, autumn sounds;
The smell of trees,
Flowers, and falling leaves
Will form memories to retrieve.

Experiences of the past
Stir among the senses' paths
And become part of creation's immortal mask.

Wondrous thought,
Reason, and conversation will soon appear
As creation's vocal perfection nears.

Sounds that inspire humanity's throngs
Soon echo from creation's songs.

Deep within the human breast
The strings of feelings move with strains
That reach beyond mortal rest.

Reflections of unexplained propensities
Settle over woman's unimaginable creation,
And conspire in musician, artisan, and all
Untold hidden gifts
That mark life's uniqueness.

And more and more—innumerably more—
As the tiny cells mature.

WHAT WONDER WE BEHOLD
AS THE HUMAN BODY UNFOLDS
AND PREPARES TO DRAW THE BREATH LIFE KNOWS!

THIS GLORIOUS CREATION
IN WHOM ETERNAL IMAGERY IS SEEN,
INSCRIBED FOREVER WITH IMMORTAL GENES,
REACHES FAR BEYOND THE SPECTRUM WE SEE—
FAR BEYOND CHANCE'S ENTROPY—
FAR BEYOND MORTALITY'S BRIEF TIME—
FAR INTO ETERNITY—

SPEAKING ITS CONTINUUM STORY
AMONG THE CROWNS OF GLORY.

Immortal Personifiers

THE IMAGINATION AND APPRECIATION OF THE MIND
REACHES BEYOND THE MATERIAL
INTO THE UNSEEN WORLD OF BEING.

IMAGINATION CAN CONJURE THE PAST
OR OUR FUTURE PATHS.

IMAGINATION CAN WRITE A PLAY, A POEM;
COMPOSE A SYMPHONY;
INSPIRE A SCULPTURE, A PAINTING;
INVENT AND DESIGN.
IMAGINATION EXPRESSES THE INNER MIND.

IMAGINATION AND APPRECIATION
SYNONYMOUSLY RACE.
THEY REACH BEYOND THE BOUNDS
OF TIME AND SPACE.

THEY LET US FEEL THE WONDER
AS DAWN CREEPS ALONG;
EXPERIENCE THE JOY OF NATURE'S SONGS;
AND SENSE THE MAJESTY OF WHERE WE BELONG.

IMAGINATION AND APPRECIATION ARE THE
CONSCIOUSNESS OF THE INVISIBLE BEYOND.

THEY EVIDENCE MORE THAN OBLIVION AND DEATH—
THEY BREATHE AN IMMORTAL BREATH.

Improbability

I SPREAD THE DECK UPON THE TABLE,
THE CARDS UPSIDE DOWN;
ALL FIFTY-TWO WERE MIXED-UP AND STREWN AROUND.

I WONDERED WHAT THE CHANCE WOULD BE,
FOR ME,
TO PICK THEM UP, ONE EACH TIME,
IN THEIR CORRECT-SUIT SEQUENCE-KIND—

ONE CHANCE IN TEN TO THE SIXTY-EIGHTH
FORMS THE IMPOSSIBLE EQUATION—
ENORMOUS ODDS, WITH ZERO EXPECTATIONS.

A NUMBER GREATER THAN ALL THE SANDS
UPON THE SHORES AND DESERTS COMBINED;
ODDS GREATER THAN THE NUMBER OF SECONDS
ESTIMATED BEFORE THE UNIVERSE'S BEGINNING TIME.

ODDS SO GREAT WE COULD NEVER,
IN ALL EARTH'S TIME,
RANDOMLY PICK THE CARDS UP
WITH ANY ORDER IN MIND.

THEN I LOOKED INTO MOLECULAR BIOLOGY
AND EXAMINED A TINY MOLECULE,
MADE UP OF NUMBERS, TOO,
TO SEE IF I COULD GLIMPSE
INTO ITS STRUCTURAL CLUES.
HEMOGLOBIN WAS THE MOLECULE I PURSUED.

I EXAMINED ITS MINUTE COMPLEXITY:
FIVE HUNDRED SEVENTY-FOUR AMINO ACIDS
ARRANGED SPECIFICALLY TO FORM ITS CHAIN.

OF THE NUMEROUS PERMUTATIONS
THESE AMINOS COULD FORM,
ONLY ONE COULD BE HEMOGLOBIN'S NORM.

TEN THOUSAND-PLUS ATOMS
WITHIN EACH MOLECULE DWELL;
NUMEROUS OF THESE COMPLEX MOLECULES RESIDE
IN EACH RED BLOOD CELL;
ONE HUNDRED SIXTY TRILLION RED CELLS
ONE PINT FILLS.

THIS INCREDIBLE FORMULATION—A MOLECULAR LUNG—
ORGANIZED TO PROVIDE OXYGEN TO EACH LIVING CELL,
AND THEN TO DELIVER THE RESIDUE
FOR US TO EXHALE.

TEN TO THE SIX HUNDREDTH AND FIFTIETH
IS THE NUMBER OF POSSIBLE PERMUTATIONS
OF AMINOS IN HEMO'S CHAIN;
AGAIN, ONLY ONE WILL MAKE A HEMOGLOBIN FRAME.

IF THESE AMINOS WERE SHUFFLED EVERY SECOND
THROUGH ALL COSMIC YEARS,
HEMOGLOBIN'S FORM
COULD NEVER SPONTANEOUSLY APPEAR.

AND WHAT OF THE ENVIRONMENT
HEMOGLOBIN REQUIRES?
AND THE LARGER, MORE COMPLEX ORGANISMS FOUND:

Plants, animals, and the numerous creatures
In life's plan?
And man, with his indefinable mind—
His capacity for art, philosophy, reason,
And conversation.

Mathematically, as the cards revealed,
There is not enough time in the universe
For chance to organize
Even the smallest biological birth.

Nature and earth alone could never mutate
In their time frame
The variety of life they claim.

How easily our folly revealed!
How quickly our wisdom stilled!

As we examine the complexities of life
And search the immensity of space,
We discover the tracks
The Creator has left to trace. [16]

Life

Like the mineral-laden, barren moon,
The earth—
Once a desolate, empty, lifeless tomb!

Between its chemicals, minerals,
And the simplest living cells,
There loomed a chasm,
Vast and absolute,
Beyond the reach
Of elements to breach.

From whence came this life?
Whence began the Sculptor's hand
To work this mystery upon the land?

No atom, mineral, or element ever brought
An idea or formed a thought;
Whereas life created from these elements
A living soul,
The human race,
And nature's magnificence upon earth's face.

Matter is compelled by life's mastery
To sculpture, shape, and trace
The designs in every leaf—
The flowers, fruits, and forest greens,
Humans, animals, birds and all living things.

Life replicates itself,
Expresses its mind,
Multiplies and replenishes after its kind,
And reveals the majesty of design.

From the mountain lakes,
Meadows, and rolling hills
To the desert's golden-rust as evening stills,
Life touches, paints, and fills;
From dust it builds.

Then life subsides and seems to die
As once again unto dust
It lays the elements aside.

From whence it comes and goes—
Who can know the secrets it bestows?

Life's Continuum

I WALKED DOWN A ROAD EARLY ONE SPRING DAY
AND SAW NEW LIFE EVERYWHERE ON DISPLAY.

IN SUMMERTIME I CAME BACK BY
TO SEE LIFE'S FRUITS GROWING HIGH.

THEN CAME FALL, AND I CHANCED TO RETURN
TO SEE THE HARVEST TURN.

WHEN WINTER WINDS BEGAN TO BLOW
I SLOWLY STROLLED A SNOWY ROAD,
WHERE LYING BENEATH SNOW-COVERED FIELDS
WAS THE RESTFUL LIFE THE WHITENESS SHIELDS,
WAITING FOR SPRING TO ARRIVE
AND, ONCE AGAIN, REVIVE.

NATURE NEVER DIES.
SHE, DEATH DEFIES.
ON LIFE'S CONTINUUM WE TOO CAN RELY.

Life's Covering

As all nature grows,
So life goes,
From the tiny seed
To the measure of the soul.

And as the winter comes,
With its covering of snow,
It hides all life
Beneath its frosty blows.

Still deep within
The covered soil
Is new-born life
Waiting to show.

So also the life we know,
As it begins to go,
Has within its covering
Life forever aglow.

Life's Elsewhere Beginnings

ALL LIFE AROUND US FOCUSES
ON ELSEWHERE BEGINNINGS
AND PERSONIFIES GENES OF ENDLESS AGES.

UNBREACHABLE INERT MATTER
SUDDENLY EXPLODES
WHEN THE MYSTERY OF LIFE
MIXES WITH ITS ATOMS,
AND THREADS ITS INVISIBLE MATTER
AMONG THE ELEMENTS OF EARTH
CAUSING THEIR BIOLOGICAL BIRTH.

THROUGH ITS SPECIFIC CHEMICAL CHAINS
LIFE REPRODUCES ITS KIND,
PATTERNING EXACTLY THE IMMORTAL MIND,
AND IMBUES ITS WONDROUS TOUCH
OF ORGANIZED BEAUTY
AS IT MULTIPLIES
ITS PRECISE PATTERNS OF GLORY.

LIFE SURPASSES ALL UNDERSTANDING
AS IT MANIFESTS ITS INVISIBLENESS
IN BIOLOGICAL MAJESTY.

Life's Voice

I SPEAK UNTO THEE
THROUGH THE MANIFESTATIONS YOU SEE;
THEY ARE EVERYWHERE—
ON LAND, IN SKIES, AND IN SEAS.

I SPEAK UNTO THEE
FROM THE HEART OF ALL HUMAN BEINGS;
FROM ALL ANIMATION, I SING.

EVERYTHING BEAUTIFUL HATH MY SOUL;
ALL NATURE BY ME DOTH GROW.

COMMUNICATION, REASON, PERCEPTION,
AND THOUGHT ARE ME,
WHICH I GIVE FREELY UNTO THEE.

WHAT DRIVES THE CONSCIOUSNESS OF THINGS,
IF NOT ME?
CANST THOU SEE MY IMMORTALITY?

AND WHAT LEAVES
WHEN THE ELEMENTS YOU HOLD TURN COLD?

WHAT MORE HOPE COULD I GIVE?
WHAT MORE PROOF THAT I LIVE?

LET MY SWEEPING VISUAL PRESENCE
SPEAK ITS IRREFUTABLE IMMORTAL EVIDENCE

AND BELIEVE IN THE LIFE YOU SEE—
AND IN IMMORTALITY.

The Master Painter

Above the timberline trees,
The tundra slopes, the rugged rocks
And mountain tops;

The streams and rivers,
And their ever-changing trails
As they mark their way
Through the hills and dales;

The newness of spring
And the life it brings;

The summer's gentle warmth, and greens;
The harvest's colors and autumn scenes;

The winter snows and frosty blows;
The covered fields and leafless groves;

The desert's golden browns,
Its rusty hues, cactus blooms
And wind-blown dunes;

The rolling clouds and storms;
The rainbow's welcome reprieves;
The thundering waves and majestic seas

Are the ever changing canvases
The Master Painter leaves.

The Materials of Life

The unseen materials of life's abundance
Represent another reality
Of a more-refined substance.

Its presence is evident to behold,
And is personified in the animation
Of its physical abode.

Though clearly visible through its effects,
It remains invisible, a paradox complex.

Sometime in the distant future
When its refinement becomes visible
And within our control,
We will understand life's relationship
To these physical elements below.

Molecular Link

THE CHEMICAL RIBBONS OF MORTAL HEREDITY,
WITH THEIR DNA MOLECULES
AND NUMEROUS GENES,
HOLD THE BLUEPRINT OF LIFE.

UNDEVIATING, THEIR RECORD SURVIVES
AND INSCRIBES.

WITH SPECIFIC PURPOSE,
WHEN CALLED UPON BY FERTILE UNION,
THE GENES WORK THEIR MIRACLE OF LIFE.

WITH MAJESTIC WONDER
THEY REPRODUCE THEIR PATTERNS.

THE BEAUTY OF THEIR PERFORMANCE
IS OF UNEQUALED GLORY
AS CONSISTENTLY THEY WHISPER
LIFE'S CONTINUUM STORY.

TELEOLOGICALLY THEY SPEAK
IN THEIR BIOLOGICAL BIRTH.

SOMEWHERE BEYOND THE CELL'S
MOLECULAR WORLD—
BEYOND ITS GENETIC MESSAGE—
SOMEWHERE BEYOND THE VISIBLE,
WE WILL FIND OUR ANCESTRAL ROOTS.

SOMEWHERE BEYOND THE FINITE,
WE WILL DISCOVER A FINAL, UNIFYING THEORY.[17]

SOMEWHERE IN THE UNSEEN WORLD,
WE WILL DISCOVER OUR LINK
WITH IMMORTALITY.

Mutation?

"BRING YE FORTH AFTER YOUR KIND,"
WAS THE ORDER OF ANCIENT TIME.

AND AS WE SEARCH THE FOSSIL MASS,
IN AGES PAST,
WE FIND FEW DEVIATIONS FROM SPECIES' KIND.

NUMEROUS UPON NUMEROUS
INTERMEDIARIES WOULD BE FOUND
IF MUTATION WERE SCIENTIFICALLY SOUND.

STILL, WE SEARCH THE WORLD
FOR THE MISSING LINKS TO UNFURL,

AND SCAVENGE AMONG GRAVES LONG-SEALED,
HOPING TO FIND INTERMEDIARIES REVEALED.

SOME OCCASIONAL SHOUTS
OF IMAGINATION ROAR,
WHEN ODD FINDS ARE SCORED.

SOME TRY TO FORCE TRANSITIONS HERE AND THERE,
BUT WHERE IS THE NEEDED EVIDENCE, WHERE?

IF MANKIND AND ALL CREATION
MUTATED FROM SINGLE CELLS,
THE FOSSIL RECORD WOULD BE RIFE
WITH EVIDENCE OF TRANSITIONAL LIFE.

But alas, the silent past is breached only
By the fantasies we feign,
Not the evidence obtained.

Never do species mutate beyond their kind!
Never the needed intermediaries will we find!

What is discovered is invariable consistency,
Immutable stasis,
With species never crossing their line.

Ants to ants!
Plants to plants!
With never a deviant.

Dinosaurs don't turn into birds,
And animals always stay within their herds;
Mutation of species never occurs.

Nor does life spontaneously emerge,
As claims the sophist's words.

Improvements within breed and seed,
But bringing forth only their kind—
Always, always, since ancient times.

The magnificence of the birds of air,
Their invariant avian lungs
And feathers rare!

The beauty of the animal breeds,
With their wild, unfurled, purebred steeds!

THE OCEAN CASTE!
THE WHALES AND FISH
AND THEIR UNALTERABLE PAST!

THE WONDERS OF NATURE,
WITH ITS TREES AND LEAVES
AND IMMUTABLE SEEDS!

THE FLOWERS THAT COVER THE EARTH!
THE GLORY OF CONSISTENT BIRTH!

DESIGN AND PURPOSE ABOUND ALL AROUND,
WHILE NATURE AND LIFE
OBEY CREATION'S RESOLUTE MIND—
"BRING YE FORTH AFTER YOUR KIND." [18]

The Mystery of Life

THE MYSTERY OF LIFE,
SO OVERWHELMING TO THE HUMAN MIND,
IS SO ILLUSIVE, IMPONDERABLE, AND REFINED.

FROM THE INNATE MINERALS OF EARTH
SUDDENLY COMES BIOLOGICAL BIRTH.

FROM LIFELESSNESS, SOON
BEAUTY AND VARIETY MYSTERIOUSLY BLOOM.

ALL OF NATURE'S WONDERS BEGIN TO APPEAR,
GROW, BLOSSOM, AND PROPAGATE OUR SPHERE.

CREATURES TOO NUMEROUS TO DEFINE
FAITHFULLY REPRODUCE THEIR KIND.

FROM THE WOMAN'S FERTILE FIELDS
EMERGE TRILLIONS OF LIVING CELLS,
COMBINING THE WONDER OF THE HUMAN SOUL.

DEPENDENTLY THEY HAVE GROWN
TO RUN, DANCE, AND SING;
TO WEEP, IMAGINE, AND DREAM;
TO COMMUNICATE WITH OTHERS;
TO CREATE, DESTROY, HATE, LOVE,
AND DISCOVER.[19]

Scientific reasoning and the intellectual mind
Can describe and define the wonders of life.
But, as to the spark
That animates living things,
Science has never
Opened the secrets of its being.

Life descends upon the earth
Like the rays of the morning sun.
Mysteriously it comes,
And, in likeness, sets when its day is done,

Ebbing elsewhere its way
To greet another dawn—another day!

Mystery Unlocked

Of all the mysteries
That envelop the universe,
None remain more hidden
Than life's biological birth.

Man's intelligence and wisdom
Remain mute to its dominion.

As death descends
Upon biological life,
And leaves its traces benign behind,
Therein lies life's secret to find.

For once death's door is unlocked,
Dispelled, then, the mystery
Life has brought.

Nature's Witness

"Earth's crammed with heaven and every common
bush afire with God." ELIZABETH BARRETT BROWNING

FROM THE FLOWING, GROWING STREAMS
THAT WIND THEIR WAY TO THE TRANQUIL BAYS;

FROM THE TALL, ARCHING, WIND-BLOWN TREES;
FROM THE MOUNTAINS AND MAJESTIC SEAS;

FROM THE WAVING GRASS OF THE ROLLING HILLS
AND THE FLOWERS IN THE MEADOW FIELDS;

FROM THE THUNDERING SOUNDS
OF THE BILLOWING CLOUDS;
FROM THE VARIETY OF NATURE'S CROWDS;

FROM THE SMALLEST CREATURE AND TINIEST FLOWER,
TO THE MAGNIFICENCE OF NATURE'S DOWER;

COMES THE THEOPHANY THAT STIRS
IMMORTAL VISION WITHIN,
AND SHOUTS THE DEMISE OF SOPHISTIC DIN.

Old Man's Farewell

For many years I've worked my way
Through the exciting times of my mortal stay.

I've seen many changes displayed;
Many marvels have happened in my day.

The majesty of the railroads;
The mighty engines and their loads;

A hundred cars, all combined,
With smoke and steam going down the line.

They had a mystic of their own;
Now in museums of history shown.

Grand Central Station, the busy crowds,
The rumbling echoes—echoes now!

I remember the first motor vehicles:
Cars, trucks, coupes, and pickups.

The changes from horse-drawn plows
And hand-milked cows!

Buildings, bridges, and machines—
What marvels human inventions bring!

COMMUNICATIONS, TELEPHONES, FAXES,
COMPUTERS, AND MEDICAL ADVANCES!

I'VE SEEN AIRPLANES AND FLYING MACHINES,
FROM PROPS TO THE ROARING JET STREAMS.

MEN ON THE MOON AND IN SPACE,
ADVENTURES AND CHANGES AT EPIC PACE!

THE MIGHTY CHANGE IN SHIPS AT SEA
AND MARITIME THINGS HAVE BEEN MINE TO SEE.

I'VE SEEN MORE NEW THINGS IN MY LIFETIME
THAN IN SIX THOUSAND YEARS OF MANKIND.

WHY ARE THE DREAMS OF THESE INVENTIONS
COMING NOW TO OUR ATTENTION?

WERE ETERNAL SECRETS HIDDEN?
UNTIL NOW WERE THEY FORBIDDEN?

SOMEDAY, WE MAY KNOW
WHY THIS LATTER-DAY SHOW.

BUT I HAVE A FEELING I'LL SOON GO
TO A PLACE WHENCE ALL THESE MIRACLES FLOW.

AND AS I LEAVE THIS EARTHLY HOME OF MINE,
I'M ABOUT TO SEE A MORE PROGRESSIVE TIME.

I HAVE A FEELING THAT I WILL WALK
AMONG CREATIONS BEYOND MY THOUGHTS.

THE MAJESTY HERE IS BUT A REFLECTION
OF ETERNAL THINGS—SOURCE OF ALL DREAMS.

WHAT AN EXCITING LIFE IT HAS BEEN,
AND IT'S ABOUT TO START ALL OVER AGAIN!

Organization

ORGANIZATION AND BEAUTY NEVER EMERGE
FROM CHAOS OR CHANCE,
WHERE ONLY CONFUSION
AND DISORGANIZATION OCCUR.

BEAUTY AND MEANINGFUL VARIETY
COME NOT FROM CHANCE'S ENTROPY.

PEOPLE WITH THEIR LOOKS, TEARS, FEARS,
AND WONDROUS MINDS,
ALSO NATURE'S FINDS,
SPRING FROM GENES OF ELSEWHERE'S PEERS;

DESCENDING GENERATIONS
FROM BILLIONS OF YEARS,
FROM REFINED MATERIALS
THAT EMANATE DEITY'S KIND,
WITH PURPOSE AND DESIGN;
ENDURING THROUGH ALL TIME.

Patience

In our quiet, more-reminiscent times, there is a feeling—
a longing— that swells within and speaks volumes of our
immortal future.

The cosmos whispers patience
To its restless crowds;
Line upon line its treasure allows.

Its unseen reasoning
Resounds beyond mortal bounds,
Speaking volumes of knowledge and meaning.

Forever flowing, wordless knowing
Swells within as its fullness begins
Opening upon us like flowers
Before the morning sun,
Quietly confirming our future to come;

Perceptually distilling upon our minds
Omnipotent thought to ponderously define.

"What a little of all we know is said." [20]

Patterns

Since distant, immeasurable time
Creation's immutable patterns
Have reflected their kind.

The seeds of moist earth,
The biological species of molecular birth,
Replicate themselves
From the genes that have been;
Their kind mysteriously huddles within.

Each an analogous portrayal;
Each a cosmic reflection;
Each a reoccurring vista
Speaking its immortal mind;
Each, among the countless windows,
Viewing their shadowed kind.

The mystical, graceful earth
Moves not alone in the boundless universe.

Nor is the wondrous human race
Alone in the immensity of space.

All entities of creation
Are permanently etched and scribed,
Ever alive,
In the endless journey
Among the patterns of time.

Pensive Thought

During quiet times, when reminiscence works
upon atheistic thought, there must be moments when
hope finds its place in memory's folds.

WHEN PENSIVE THOUGHT
RUMBLES THROUGH THE FAITHLESS DROUGHT,
AND REMINISCENCE QUIETLY STIRS ABOUT,
THERE HEAPS UPON THE AGNOSTIC MIND
THE WONDERMENT OF DOUBT.

WHEN THE CONFLICT OF LOVE'S FOREVER-HOLD
RUMMAGES AMONG FOND MEMORY'S FOLDS,
THERE OPENS CREVICES EVER SO SMALL,
FOR IMMORTALITY'S DISQUIETING RAYS TO FALL,

WHERE ATHEISTIC PARADIGMS
ERODE AND RUST,
AND CRUMBLE INTO DUST.

Philosophic Knowledge

ALL AROUND, MAN'S KNOWLEDGE IS LEFT WANTING
AS NIHILISM IS PURSUED.

ROOTED AND EARTH-BOUND, ONLY TO SPROUT,
THEN WITHER MEANINGLESS
IN A FAITHLESS DROUGHT.

CHAINED TO THE LIMITS OF MORTALITY,
CROWNING ITS FINAL THEORY
WITH THE AMBIGUITY OF CHANCE,

MAN'S FATED KNOWLEDGE
IS DRAWN ON A BARREN DRAY
ONLY TO COLLAPSE INTO OBLIVIOUS DECAY.

Ponderous Evidence

THE SPIRIT OF LIFE,
FOLLOWING ITS MATING CALLS,
SWEEPS OVER THE ELEMENTS OF EARTH
AND WHISPERS THEIR BIOLOGICAL BIRTH.

WITH OBEDIENCE UNKNOWN TO MORTAL INTELLIGENCE,
LIFE INFUSES, IMBUES, AND ANIMATES THE ELEMENTS.

NOT BY ANY HUMAN HAND,
NOR THE DIRECTION OF MAN;
ONLY BY THE GIFT OF ETERNAL COMMAND
DO THE ELEMENTS UNDERSTAND,
FOLLOW, AND FORMULATE LIFE'S SPECIFIC PLAN.

LIFE, CREATION'S EMPIRICAL PROOF,
IS PONDEROUS EVIDENCE
OF A CREATOR'S PRESENCE.

Purpose

When we think of space ever-extending,
Of time never-ending,
The captured and controlled
Energy of atoms,

The unnumbered universes
And countless stars,
This wondrous earth of ours,
The mystery of light,
The majesty of night,
The reign of law and order,
And the enormous energy
In celestial might; [21]

We bow in humble reverence
To how little we know
Of the glory bestowed in our cosmic show.

In thunderous manifestation
Eternity roars its visual shouts!
The evidence is beyond doubt
That design and purpose surround us about.

We are an integral part
Of this theophany of divine design!

The human race, nature, and all of life
Could not be an accident in time.

69

Reason

All earthly creations
Bow in humble submission
To man's dominion.

Man alone has the gift of reason.
He alone can plan, direct,
And affect his seasons.

Why then—with all the visual evidence
Of a directing presence,

In the midst of chance's predictable course
Toward chaos and confusion,

In clear view of the multitudinous witnesses
Of nature's specificity and purpose,

With the evidence of mathematical improbability
Against evolutionary theory
Defined so clearly—

Can humanity think itself as naught
And assign oblivion to its lot?

How can a rational people
Say final good-byes
And think themselves to permanently die?

Receding Faith

AN EMPTINESS
SPREADS ACROSS THE OCEAN SANDS
AS THE EBBING TIDES
RECEDE THEIR ROCKY MOORINGS.

A QUIETNESS ECHOES WITH SADNESS [22]
AS FAITH LETS GO ITS MOORINGS
LEAVING HUMANITY ALONE, COLD, AND NUMB,
UPON LIFE'S LONELY SHORES.

BUT ALONENESS DOES NOT LAST FOREVER.
WITH ITS INTIMATE, RESTFUL ASSURANCE,
THE SEA RETURNS AGAIN ITS THUNDEROUS ROARS.

SO IMMORTAL HOPE, IN TIME,
RUSHES IN AGAIN
TO DROWN THE SOPHISTRY OF BARREN THOUGHT,
AND RESTORE FAITH'S RAPPORT ONCE MORE.

The Sculptor's Hand

FROM MARBLE
CUT AWAY IN A QUARRY HILL,
MICHELANGELO CARVED AWAY STONE
UNTIL HE REVEALED BEAUTY WITHIN—
HIS DAVID—
MAJESTIC, SERENE, ALONE.

SO, BY THE MASTER SCULPTOR'S HAND,
FROM THE ELEMENTS
IS FORMED A WOMAN—A MAN.

NOT A FROZEN IMAGE IN STONE,
NOR A LIFELESS SCULPTURE HONED;

BUT A LIVING SOUL,
A MICHELANGELO,
A DAVID, KING OF ISRAEL.

Secrets Revealed

We will someday discover the physical properties of immortal matter.

UNTIL THE LIGHT OF DISCOVERY BEGAN TO UNFURL,
THE MYSTERIES OF THE BIOLOGICAL WORLD
KEPT THEIR SECRETS STILL.

SO ALSO THE INVISIBLE MATTER
THAT BRINGS ELEMENTS ALIVE
WILL, SOMEDAY, IN UNDERSTANDING THRIVE.

REVEALING THEN THE MYSTERY OF BIOLOGICAL BIRTH,
AND LIFE'S POWER OVER THE ELEMENTS OF EARTH;

REVEALING THEN THE MYSTERY OF DEATH,
NOW HIDDEN IN THE REAPER'S BREATH;

REVEALING THEN THE MYSTERY OF PROPENSITIES,
THE SECRETS OF NATURE'S INSTINCTS,
OF GENIUS AND TALENT;

REVEALING THEN THE SOURCE
OF REASON AND THOUGHT,
AND THE PURPOSE MORTALITY HAS BROUGHT;

REVEALING THEN THE IMMORTAL SOUL,
ITS EVERLASTING IDENTITY AND INFINITE GOALS.

So Near, So Far Away

HUMANITY IS ON THE BRINK OF TRUTH,
SO NEAR ITS WATER'S EDGE—
FLOUNDERING,
EVER-SHIFTING, DRIFTING, WANDERING.

TRUTH LINGERS HIDDEN FROM TANGIBLE VIEW,
PATIENTLY WAITING TO BE PURSUED.

TO DREAM OF BOUNDS BEYOND—
TO FEEL THE HOPE THAT FUTURE LONGS—

TO FLY WITH REALISTIC DREAMS
TO HEIGHTS UNSEEN—

TO EXAMINE WITH RATIONAL THOUGHT
THE PURPOSE MORTALITY HAS BROUGHT—

IS TO LIFT THE CUP AND DRINK—
TO OPEN THE DOOR OF IMMORTALS' STORES.

TRUTH'S "FINAL THEORY"
LIES BEYOND FINITE DOORS.

Theories

THE THEORIES OF SCIENCE
ARE BUT WINDOWS OF IMAGINATION
THAT EXPOSE HUMANITY'S INTELLECT AND CURIOSITY—
CLOUDED WINDOWS
AS WE STAGER AMIDST THE MAJESTY OF OMNISCIENCE.

THEORIES EVER CHANGING,
EVER ADJUSTING,
AS THE REACHES OF KNOWLEDGE FILTER IN,
AS WE WANDER FINITE
IN THE WONDER OF IT ALL.

UNTIL WE CONSIDER IMMORTAL PURPOSE,
THE FINAL THEORY WILL NEVER UNRAVEL,
THE EQUATION WILL NEVER BE COMPLETE,
NEVER SECURE,
NEVER FULLY UNDERSTOOD.

WE RACE TO KEEP THE VISIBLE EVIDENCE
EVER BEFORE US,
NEVER STOPPING TO LET THE DAWN
OF TRANSCENDENTAL VIEWS FILTER UPON US.

LIKE THE LIGHT AFTER A NIGHT OF DARKNESS,
THE FINER ELEMENTS OF THE UNSEEN
AWAIT TO BE DISCOVERED—
WAITING FOR HUMANITY TO OPEN ITS SHADES.

To Be There

To be there when they come,
These atheistic ones;

To be there when their life is done,
As they catch the folly
Of their philosophic run.

I wonder what then they'll say
When they touch eternal belief
And their teachings crumble
In desperate grief.

Embarrassment, shame, and regret
For the falsehoods they begat!

Their wisdom gone!
Their philosophies proven wrong!

Now too late to change
Their well-worn text,
Laced with fraud and defects,
Yet left as though correct.

What humiliation to them
When they come,
These babbling atheistic ones.

To Know

THE SWEEPING PANORAMA
OF EVIDENTIAL VISTAS
THAT WORK UPON PENSIVE THOUGHT
STEERS THE REASONING MIND
TOWARD LIFE'S CONTINUUM DESTINY.

BUT TO FEEL IMMORTAL CERTAINTY,
TO KNOW WITH CALMING ASSURANCE,
COMES ONLY FROM THE EPOCH NATURE
OF DEITY SPEAKING CONFIRMING SOUNDS
TO THE KINSHIP OF THE SOUL.

UNDIMINISHED BY LANGUAGE,
OR LEARNING, OR STATUS,
THIS UNSPEAKABLE SYMPHONY
RESOUNDS CONVICTION
FOR THE HUMBLE WANDERER TO KNOW.[23]

Veritable Story

As I hear the strains of nature's thunder
And feel the gentle breeze
Sweeping the prairie trees;

And behold creation's wonders,
Its rivers and flowing streams,
The desert's golden-browns,
And the forest's greens;

As I hear the ocean's waves,
And view the sculptured caves,
And walk upon the sands of ageless days;

I feel immortality's physical expressions
Flooding over me;

Its eternal tides rolling in
From unseen seas;

Dispensing its glory,
Confirming its veritable story.

Who Am I?

Who am I
Among the innumerable, numbered known,
Who have trodden the dust of my home?

Why am I
Upon this speck of dust,
Circling among the countless stars,
In the vast, cosmic wilderness?

The answers come
As specificity lays its purpose upon reason.

Consider the sun, the moon, and the earth,
And how they travel
Their predetermined courses,
Perfectly aligned, and chemically combined
To provide life's continual birth.

Consider the oceans and seas,
And how they send their moisture
Over the valleys and mountain tops
To the flora leaves;
Then, in wondrous beauty,
Bring it back again
Through rivers and flowing streams.

Endlessly and harmoniously
The earth, the moon, and the sun
Roll upon their wings,
Faithfully maintaining a home for living things.

WHERE AM I?
UPON AN EARTH
WHERE EXISTENCE RESOUNDS WITH PURPOSE!

WHO AM I
WITH INWARD EMOTIONS REACHING BEYOND CHANCE,
WITH THE CAPACITY FOR JOY, APPRECIATION,
THOUGHT, IMAGINATION, AND ROMANCE?

WHO AM I
WHO CAN APPRECIATE
THE BEAUTY OF THE NIGHTLY STARS,
THE MOON'S SUBTLE DELIGHTS,
THE FLORA-COVERED LANDS, THE MAJESTIC SEAS,
THE RIVERS AND TREES, AND THE QUIET BREEZE?

WHO AM I
WHO CAN COMPREHEND
THE COLORS OF NATURE'S FLOWERS,
THE MYSTICAL RAIN SHOWERS,
THE MAJESTIC FLIGHT OF BIRDS,
THE PUREBRED GALLOPING HERDS,
AND MORE AND MORE AS THE EMOTIONS STIR?

WHO AM I?
SOMEONE WITHIN WHOM REVERENCE, CHARACTER,
MORALITY, AND INSPIRATION EXCELS;
SOMEONE WITHIN WHOM
THE ATTRIBUTES OF THE INVISIBLE DWELLS.

WHO AM I?
THE IMAGE OF ELSEWHERE'S GENES;
THE SPARK OF INTELLIGENCE SUPREME;
FAR MORE THAN CAN BE SEEN.

Windows

As we live our earthly lives,
Shaded from reality's view,
Where we see only dimly-lit versions
From our windowless excursions,
Little wonder we're surprised
When glimpses of eternity arise.

Look around, doubting friend,
Eternity is open to view.
Its windows are there—though seen by few;
Its shades are closed only by you.

Eternal rays are only as bright
As our perceptive sight.

Catch a glimpse of ocean sand—
Hold a song-bird in your hand—
Listen to nature's births—
The flowers, trees and life on earth
All speak eternal worth.

Still, many lock the windows shut
Preferring to live in deist philosophical rut
Where they feebly attempt to deny
Everything heaven-sent;
And where lust and worldly things
Fight every view heaven brings.

Foolish man, dust off the unbelief
From your philosophical briefs,
And let the evidence
Instill its confirming peace.

Epilogue

THE UNHAPPY EPILOGUE OF EVOLUTION
IS DESOLATION, DISINTEGRATION, AND DARKNESS
AS ITS ANIMATED MATTER
PASSES INTO DISORDER, DIFFUSION, AND DEATH.

EVOLUTION'S EARTH,
AS IT ACCIDENTLY ROLLS UPON ITS DECLINING COURSE,
AS IT SUCCUMBS TO THE FORCES OF FRICTION,
AS IT DISSIPATES ITS ENERGY,
IS TO BECOME A CHAOTIC THEATER OF DECAY,
A GLOOMY DRAMA OF IRREVERSIBLE DEGRADATION
TO BE RESOLVED INTO DUST, [24]
THEN TUMBLE OVER THE PRECIPICE OF OBLIVION—

FROM INERT TO INERT—IS EVOLUTION'S EARTH—
WITH A BRIEF INTERVAL
OF THE MOST DYNAMIC DEMONSTRATION
OF INTELLIGENCE, DESIGN, BEAUTY, AND SPECIFICITY
EVER EXPERIENCED BY ELEMENTAL SUBSTANCE.

THIS THEOPHANY OF COSMIC GLORY
WITHOUT THOUGHT OR PURPOSE—

THIS PROFUSION OF SPECIFICITY AND DESIGN
THE RESULT OF MINDLESS CHANCE—

THERE IS ANOTHER SOUND,
ANOTHER EPILOGUE
THAT WHISPERS A DIFFERENT REFRAIN—

One more rational,
Far more believable and reasonable,
A message of transcendental purpose.

Life with all its glory and obvious design,
Its unexplainable molecular specificity,
Its resounding message of purpose,
Will never resolve into endless, breathless dust.

Life demonstrates a position firmly secure
Beyond the reaches of chance—
Beyond our mortal demise—
Beyond nihilism's delusive charade.

Beyond the sound of the sophist's serenade
Is quite a different refrain.

Evolution's epilogue of nothing
Is not the sound the cosmos whispers.

Part Two

Thoughts

to Consider

Accountability

Listen to the eerie wind
As it threatens retribution
Upon the wayward throngs,
Avenging their wrongs.

Listen to its warning sounds
As it whispers along.

Only goodness and probity
Can hedge the mournful cry.

So listen to its stirrings
As they billow in conduct's sky—
Listen, you passersby.

Anomaly's Cry

I FEEL STRANDED ON A TROUBLED SEA
WITH NO ONE THERE, BUT ME.

I WISH I WERE WHOLE
LIKE OTHERS I KNOW.

IF ONLY I COULD WALK AS OTHERS WALK,
AND SEE AS OTHERS SEE;
IF ONLY I COULD TALK AS OTHERS,
AND BE WITHOUT ANOMALIES.

WHY MUST I SUFFER SO
FOR SOMETHING BEYOND MY CONTROL?

PLEASE, HELP ME DURING THIS BRIEF TIME,
UNTIL MY TROUBLES ARE FAR BEHIND.

YOUR COMPASSION AND LOVING CARE,
AND THE TIME YOU SPARE,
WILL CARRY ME ON MY UPWARD FLIGHT
TO WHERE EVERYTHING WILL BE ALL RIGHT.

THEN, TOGETHER WE'LL LOOK BACK
THROUGH TIME'S PORTHOLES
AND VIEW YOUR DEVOTIONAL SOUL,
WHERE WORDS WILL NOT BE KNOWN
TO EXPRESS MY FEELINGS
FOR THE LOVE YOU'VE SHOWN.

Binding Ties

Stooped and shuffling,
He holding her hand—
With the beauty of youth gone—
These two wander along.

Clothing hangs loosely
Over their withered frames—
The sturdiness of youth discarded
Where unsteadiness remains.

Voices are shaky and words slowly said;
Years of memories have fled.
Devotion and duty enwrap
These weathered friends.

Their gentle gaze reaches endlessly beyond.
Nourished by the years gone,
Their weakness and feebleness
Strengthens the inseparable bond.

Love begins to be understood
As they shuffle along;
Its meaning with these belongs.

Sentiment grows
As age nourishes their souls.

When absence bereaves a time,
Each follows, the other to find.

Canine Friend

Like the dew of dawn
Our friend is gone.

Now memories only, his playful streaks,
As years he ran his beat.

He traveled through our sentiments,
Saddened when we'd leave,
Our journey to proceed;

But always remembering when,
Each time, we'd return again.

Many sorrows and troubles would end,
Many wounds he would mend,
As faithfully our needs he would attend,
This canine friend.

There was always contentment around
Wherever he was found.

But now, his winter has come;
He silently crept away today,
Quietly to stay.

A Child's Wants

I WANT MOTHER AND FATHER NEAR,
TO LEND A LISTENING EAR
AND TAKE AWAY MY FEARS.

I WANT OTHERS AROUND THE HOUSE,
CHILDREN, LIKE ME, TO PLAY AND ROUSE.

WHEN I GO AWAY TO SCHOOL OR PLAY,
I WANT SOMEONE HOME WHEN I COME IN TO STAY.

I NEED A HOME WHERE PARENTS RESIDE,
WHERE I CAN FEEL SECURE INSIDE.

I NEED SOMEONE TO CARE FOR ME,
I NEED A FAMILY.

I'M NOT ASKING A LOT OF YOU,
IF YOU WERE A CHILD,
YOU WOULD WANT IT TOO.

I HOPE I REMEMBER THESE NEEDS I SEE
SO WHEN I HAVE CHILDREN,
THEY CAN COUNT ON ME.

Choices

I wonder as I begin life's run,
With its courses to pursue
And its challenges to be won,
Where I'll be when the race is done.

Some roads are easy to follow,
While others are more difficult.
Some goals take longer to achieve,
While others are quickly built.

But on what in the end
Does the best depend?
What message does effort send?

How can I be certain which way to go?
Who will direct my efforts—who knows—
As I come to the cross roads
Which road is best for me?

Will I set aside the easy ride?
Will I strengthen and lengthen my stride?

Can I look beyond the short-term work?
Can I wait to see time's worth?

I hope, as I come to the choices to make,
It's not the easy road I'll take.

Clouding Mist

"For now we see through a glass, darkly . . ." I COR. 13:12

AS THE SUN'S DISSIPATING RAYS
MIX DAYLIGHT ALONG;

AS WE STROLL AMID THE DISTANT GLIMPSES
THAT COME AND GO
IN THE FOG'S EBB AND FLOW,
AND LIFE'S HEAVES AND THROES;

OUR VISION CATCHES DIRECTION AND CONTENTMENT,
AND CONFIRMS MEANING TO OUR BEING—
A FEELING WE BELONG.

A PURPOSE SUPPORTS AND CARRIES US
AS THE CLOUDING MIST LIFTS, ERELONG.

Conscience

Thou who rides mightily
Upon the wings of conduct,

Never from thy lofty height descend,
Never thy purpose end.

Thou canst not hide from wrong
Nor disguise haunting lies.

Our voyage, without thee,
Would be rudderless
Upon an amoral sea.

Thou catalyst to the peaceful soul,
Abide with me and let me know.

Conscience's Role

In the quiet moments
When conscience plays its role
Upon the human soul,
There awakens within, a troubling time
For deeds we've done
That conflict with the moral mind.

But conscience can rest in peace—
With change and immortal hope,
The soul can find relief.

Contagion

Our acts and thoughts
Are indelibly inscribed
In the fabric of our souls.
By contagion they bestow
The propensities we know.

Nothing lives but a moment!
All is recorded with an iron pen
To be recalled
To support our actions again.

We are the masters in control
And determine that which we know.

By contagion we wrought
The paths we walk.

Creation's Cry

FROM A TINY CELL THERE BEGINS TO GROW
A LIFE ONLY A MOTHER KNOWS—A LIVING SOUL.

THE MAJESTY OF HER ETERNAL GIFT
IS UNMATCHED IN MYSTERY'S MYTH—

HER ETERNAL IMAGERY IS FORMED
IN THE CHILD TO BE BORN.

ELEMENTS EVERLASTINGLY ALIVE
BECOME SACRED LIFE TO SURVIVE.

NO CREATION ON EARTH
EQUALS THE HUMAN BIRTH!

BUT WHEN CREATION'S POWER TURNS SOUR
BY MAN'S GENOCIDAL POWER,
AND THE MOTHERS' CREATION STILLS,
WHAT SORROW WE FEEL!

GIVER OF LIFE—CREATOR DIVINE—
PROTECT THE GLORY TO THEE ASSIGNED,

FOR WONDROUS IS THE LIFE
ENTWINED WITH THINE.

Deceived

You say you are my friend.
For how long? Until when?
Until the wind as willows bend
Your loyalties to your selfish ends?

I trusted you to guide my way
Not knowing where evil lay.

I relied on the safety of your trust,
Yet all you sought was your selfish lot;
Despair and sorrow was all I got.

I put myself in your protecting care,
But all I was to you—a foolish dare.
As cheat and liar you were there.

You are no friend of mine;
No friend would cause such moral decline,
Or sorrow, or regret, or troubling time.

Because I chose you to be a friend,
I must start all over again.

From experience's view,
Next time, I hope to find one who cares,
One more sublime,
Someone I can trust to be a friend of mine.

Deity's Presence

A PEACEFUL CALM
DISTILLS UPON THE SOULS
OF THOSE TO WHOM
THEISTIC THOUGHTS ARE KNOWN;

ASSURING THROUGH THE STORMS
OF THOUGHTLESS NORMS;

DISCERNING THROUGH THE CLOUDS
OF PHILOSOPHICAL CROWDS;

BRIGHTENING AS THE SUN
WHEN DARKNESS COMES;

DISPENSING HOPE AND PURPOSE
WHILE THE RACE IS RUN.

The Diary

Life's diary is filled with notes
Of everyday things,
Of struggles and achievements,
Of sorrows and the happiness life brings.

But most telling and revealing,
Most remembered
Are the pages where love is written in.

Early entries are often confused
By the script of fantasy's bliss—
With fleeting feelings and mistaken dealings.

True love is difficult to find and takes time.
It is inscribed over many years—
Of our joys, tears, and fears.

Scribblings of little things
Are the songs love sings.

The children of love are the binding pages
As love matures, edits, ages.
Entries would be few
Without things children do.

THE GREATEST LOVE STORIES ARE WRITTEN
AS ORDINARY EXPERIENCES BEGIN—
ANCHORED WITH DUTY AND DEVOTION—

WHERE FAMILIAL AFFECTION ENTERS IN
AND FIDELITY AND TRUST ARE WRITTEN THEREIN.

THE MEANING OF LOVE BEGINS TO UNFOLD
AS THE DIARY IS CLOSED.

Discontentment

SOME DISCONTENTMENT PROVIDES ACCESS
TO GROWTH AND PROGRESS.

SEEKING IMPROVEMENT, ACHIEVING GOALS,
AND STRIVING TO DO BETTER
ADDS PLEASURE TO LIFE'S STROLLS,
GUARANTEES PURPOSE AND DIRECTION,
AND IS THE PATHWAY TO PERFECTION.

BUT DISCONTENTMENT CAN BECOME
A HARBINGER OF GREED
UPON WHICH JEALOUSY FEEDS.

WHEN WE LONG FOR MORE AND MORE
AND ARE NEVER SATISFIED AROUND OUR DOOR,
OUR CONTENTMENT IS SOON GONE,
FOREVER SEEKING TREASURES BEYOND.

THE MORE WE SEARCH FOR MORE,
THE GREATER OUR DISCONTENTMENT SOARS.

OUR CASTLES IN THE SKY
CAN CAUSE HAPPINESS TO PASS US BY.

WE SHOULD EXPLORE WHAT WE HAVE,
BEFORE WE SEARCH SOME DISTANT SHORE.

THERE WILL COME A TIME WHEN TREASURES
WILL BE MEASURED BY SIMPLE THINGS,
NOT WEALTH'S GLIMMERINGS.

SO AS WE CHOOSE FROM AMONG LIFE'S ARRAY,
LET'S NOT THROW THE REAL TREASURES AWAY.

"Do Unto Others"

IF OUR LIVES ENTWINED FOREVER
AND THE END OF TIME WERE NEVER;

IF WE KNEW THE TIME WOULD COME
WHEN EQUALITY WAS THE NORM TO RUN;

AND WE WOULD MEET AGAIN AND AGAIN,
ALWAYS REMEMBERING WHERE WE HAD BEEN;

HOW WOULD YOU DO UNTO ME, AND I TO YOU
AS WE TRAVEL THIS LIFE THROUGH?

Earth Time

How long after my birth
Will I live here on earth?

Was I born with eternal light
Soon to take its flight,
Only to help others—
Endear their hearts—
Then leave my earthly home
And those I loved so short a time?

Or is my course
To settle scores, fight wars,
Then search for eternal shores?

Or will I live long enough
To experience many years
Of joys and mortal fears?

However long my time will be,
Or the trials and joys I may see,
Help me to leave a legacy
That will inspire those who follow me,

And with favor review my past,
Is all I ask.

Econ 101

"THOSE WHO HAVE MORE, AND SOME TO SPARE,
SHOULD BE FORCED TO PAY THEIR FAIR SHARE,"
THE CLASS OF ECON 101 DECLARED.

"WE SHOULD ABHOR THOSE WHO WANT MORE;
THERE SHOULD BE LAWS TO EVEN THE SCORE."

"TOMORROW," THE PROFESSOR PROFESSED,
"WE'LL HAVE A TEST
TO SEE IF WE CAN PUT OUR MINDS AT REST.

"SO STUDY WELL,
FOR TOMORROW WILL TELL
WHO KNOWS THE MATERIAL."

SOME STUDIED FAR INTO THE NIGHT
FOR GREATER INSIGHT.

AFTER THE TEST, AS THE SCORES WERE EXPLORED,
THEY FOUND THAT THEIR MENTOR
HAD AVERAGED THE SCORES
SO HE WOULDN'T OFFEND ANYMORE.

ALL RECEIVED A C,
RATHER THAN FAIL, OR GET AN A, B, OR D.

THERE WAS A ROAR
FROM THOSE WHO HAD STUDIED THE NIGHT BEFORE!

THE PROFESSOR DECLARED,
"I THOUGHT IT ONLY FAIR
TO SHOW THE CLASS THAT WE CARED."

THEN HE SAID,
"THERE WILL BE ANOTHER QUIZ TOMORROW,
TO SEE IF WE CAN RAISE THE SCORE SOME MORE."

THE STUDIOUS DECIDED NOT TO STUDY
IF THEY MUST AVERAGE THE SCORE AS BEFORE.

AFTER THE SECOND TEST,
WHEN THE GRADES WERE KNOWN,
THE LACK OF INCENTIVE WAS CLEARLY SHOWN.

THE AVERAGE SCORE
WAS MUCH LOWER THAN BEFORE
BECAUSE NO ONE CARED ANYMORE.

THE PROFESSOR CAREFULLY EXPLAINED
TO THE SLOTHFUL
AND THOSE WHO HAD COMPLAINED,

"WHEN YOU PUNISH INCENTIVE IN ANY ECONOMY,
YOU GUARANTEE A LOWER EQUALITY.

"INCENTIVE IS THE DRIVING FORCE
THAT ALL SUCCESS MUST ENDORSE."

OF COURSE![25]

Eternal Salute

WHEN AFTER THIS LIFE IS DONE
AND OUR TIME WITH ETERNITY HAS COME,
HOW WILL OUR MORTAL AGENCY
HAVE PLAYED UPON OUR ETERNAL QUEST?

WILL OUR ARMOR APPEAR UNSULLIED?
WILL OUR MEMORIES SWEEP US BY
THE DREGS OF A GUILTY CONSCIENCE?

WILL OUR COURSE
HAVE BEEN WELL-FOUGHT?

WILL OUR SALUTE PASS US BY
THE SENTINELS OF IMMORTALITY?

WHEN OUR ETERNAL DESTINY
LAYS ITS REALITY UPON US,
AND ACCOUNTABILITY
PRESENTS ITS LONELY RECOMPENSE,

WILL OUR MORTAL JOURNEY
CARRY US WITH DIGNITY
INTO THE TIMELESS AGES AHEAD?

Faith Like a Child

If you could know a child's mind
And its acquaintance with things divine—

If you could see with a child's eyes
Or experience its longing cries—

If you could understand how a child feels—
The secrets of faith would be revealed.

But if this faith is not nurtured,
It retreats into the caverns of the mind
Where it can be difficult to find.

There, it lingers and haunts
In the faithless drought
Waiting for pensive thought,
Reminiscence, or hope to stir about.

Then the simple faith of a child
Begins to renew,
And comes again to our rescue.

The Fall

THE HISS OF TEMPTATION'S DARE,
SO ENTICING TO THE UNAWARE,
PULLS US DOWN TO THE DEPTHS OF DESPAIR,
THEN LAUGHS WHEN WE'RE CAUGHT IN ITS SNARE.

HOW MANY HAVE GONE BEFORE?
HOW MANY HAVE TAKEN THIS PATH OF HORROR,
DECEIVED BY DELUSION'S MASK,
ONLY TO FIND A BROKEN FLASK
OF POISONOUS GAS?

HOW EASILY WE FALL!
HOW FOOLISH ALL!

YET, DEEP WITHIN THE BROKEN HEART
A FORGIVING CONSCIENCE IMPARTS HOPE,
THAT WE CAN ASCEND
FROM THE CAVERNS DEEP—
OUR DESTINY TO KEEP.

LBLEE
98

A Father's Last Words

Of all the simple words I've heard,
Those most remembered
Are the last words
My father spoke to me.

"You've been good to me.
I love you and I'm proud
Of all you do."

His words, though few,
Are indelibly inscribed in my heart and soul,
And have become a life-long goal.

I hope for nothing more
Than to be certain
That those words of praise he spoke
In the closing moments of his days,
Will be those I will hear
When we meet again someday.

Footsteps

WE SEE A CHILD
COME INTO THE WORLD—
SO DEPENDENT IN ITS EARLY YEARS!

WE FEEL THE CHILD'S NEED FOR ATTENTION,
ITS CRY FOR HELP AND DIRECTION.

SO QUICKLY THIS CHILD INHERITS
FROM ITS SURROUNDING KIN
WHATEVER THEY INSTILL WITHIN.

AS TIME COMES AND GOES,
HOW HAVE WE HELPED THIS CHILD GROW?

SO SOON THE DAYS OF YOUTH ARE GONE!
SO SOON OUR FEELINGS, HABITS, AND MORALS
TO THE FUTURE BELONG!

WHAT HAVE WE INGRAINED IN THE GENERATIONS
TO UNFOLD?
IN THIS CHILD, WHAT HAVE WE FORETOLD?

Fragments of the Past

INWARDLY, THE FRAGMENTS OF THE PAST FLICKER;
LIKE FADING EMBERS THEY GLOW.

THEIR TRACES LUSTER OUR MEMORIES,
CALLING US THROUGH THEIR DISTANT ECHOES
TO THE REFINEMENTS OF LONG AGO.

THEIR SHIELDED SOUNDS
BURN IN THE DEPTHS OF THE HUMAN SOUL.

NEVER LEAVING US ALONE,
THEIR HOPEFUL HOLD CARRIES US
ON OUR JOURNEY HOME.

Friends

While traveling the road of life,
It's important to have friends along the way.

People who care,
Who will set aside their personal pride;
Friends in whom to confide.

It's important as we come
To the hills and climbs
To find help and directing signs.

It's our friends, those who care,
Who help us find happiness somewhere.

And as we move along life's roads,
Have we been a friend to others?
Helped them carry their loads?
Pulled them up when they were down?
Gone without for those around?

Has our example and help
Led others to become more refined,
More holy, more good, more sublime?

How will our friendship be measured in time?

The Friends of Adversity

Suffering, sickness, and sorrow
Bring with them a circle of friends,
And a crown that wears well
Where time never ends.

If ever hope lies within,
It is when sickness and suffering begin.
Joy is only comprehended
As sorrow works its miracle upon men.

Health and vitality become known
As the affliction of sickness moans.

Pain can never be understood
Until its biting force is withstood.

We can never fully appreciate
The grassy sea of the spring prairie
With its countless flowers in bloom,
Or the warmth of the summer sun
Without wind's fierce breath,
Cold and numb,
As winter comes.

So, also, the friends of adversity
Acquaint us with the grief
That measures our pleasures
With the depth they bequeath.

Furnishings

We carefully select the furnishings
That we place in our homes.
We plan our decorating themes,
And coordinate the color schemes.

We take great pride in what goes inside
Where we reside.

But when it comes to our minds,
We put in everything there is to find,
Even though the furnishings of the mind
Are of a permanent kind.

What we put in
Show What our interests have been
And becomes our discipline.

It's all within our control
To sort out the bad from the good we know.
To leave the junk aside
And let only the good inside.

The furnishings of the mind
Are possessions we carry through time.
We must select them well
For they will tell
Of the person in whose house they dwell.

Gone

No longer to hear the familiar voice;
No longer to feel the tender touch;
No longer to hold who gave so much.

We wonder where hath gone the soul
From the lifeless form we behold.

The life that stirred within
Hath elsewhere to begin.

Having endeared our hearts,
Our dreams, our hopes
To another place, another time,
Where follows all mankind.

Again to hear, and touch, and see,
Where winter's death will never be.

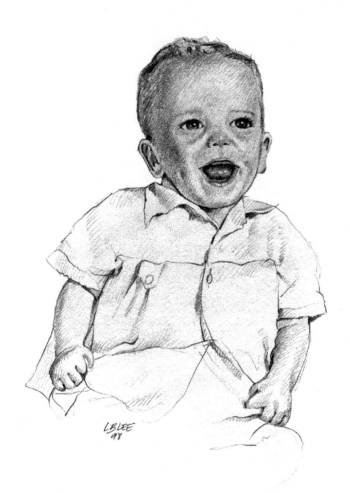

Good-bye

*In memory of our third son, Perry Lynn, who died from a
congenital heart problem when he was seven and one-half
months old.*

As we looked into your smiling face
And held your tiny hands,
We felt the joy—
The tears—
Consoled our fears—
Remembered the silent, restless nights
As you struggled for your life.

And as your evening good-bye
Gently folded over us,
With its empty, longing cry,
And wonderment of why,

Your ever-reaching eyes
Spoke hope of much more for us to know
As our journey follows where you go.

Happiness

Some look beyond their surrounding time
For happiness to find.

But happiness is not a goal,
Or a place to go,
Nor is it only for others to know.

Nor is it something intangible or far-away,
Or a thing,
Or something others bring.

Happiness is here, not some distant place.
It's how we run the race,
And embrace the challenges we face.

So make what you can
Of each day at hand—

Listen to the songs of nature's throngs;
Do some good deeds;
Help mend someone's wrongs;
Think of your brothers, sisters, others,
And their concerns—

Then you'll soon learn
That happiness is woven among
The good you've done,
And life as it's run.

History

Down through the annals of time
Rumbles the history of mankind—
Heaps of dust blown in the sands of time.

With wondrous intellect and reasoning minds,
Why the ruins, crumbled arches,
And earthen-covered remnants left behind?
Where is any lasting peace to find?

Why do civilizations expire in vain?
Why must the huddled masses lie repressed
Again and again in the blowing dune's unrest?

How long before human suffering can cease?
How long must a people live
Before they can find peace?

The answers lie in crumbled, broken stones
Trampled by desecration's storms,
Left blown and scattered by barren norms
Of hissing, venomous greed and lust
Imbued, etched in the blowing dust.

Only when the profane hisses are crushed
Will the tragedies of history be hushed.

Home

There is a yearning in the heart of everyone,
An attraction—a longing—
To go home if they can.

A place of peace and rest—of gentler times—
If only in the recesses of the mind.

A place of refuge,
The rocking chair,
Stories, love, and tender care.

Home, where there is dignity and respect,
And lack of neglect.
Where needs are met and children kept.

Where there is refuge from the storm—
A place, a feeling, safe and warm.

Where motherhood is honored and revered—
Children born and reared.

Home to the values of the past—
Fidelity, loyalty, and trust that lasts.

Where there is reverence, faith, and prayers—
Always hope—and hands held, there.

Home—where goodness and virtue are applied.
Home—where humanity can survive.

Independent People

INDEPENDENT PEOPLE NEED NO GUARANTEES
OR ENTITLEMENT FEES;
THEY CREATE THEIR OWN OPPORTUNITIES.

LEAVE THEM ALONE
AND THEIR CREATIVE POWERS WILL SOON BE SHOWN.

THEY HOLD PROGRESS IN THEIR HANDS;
IDEAS EXPAND AT THEIR COMMAND.

MIRACLES HAPPEN AS THEY BELIEVE,
BECAUSE THEY KNOW HOW TO ACHIEVE.

NEARLY EVERYTHING THAT CAUSES SOCIETY TO RUN
IS THE RESULT OF WHAT THEY HAVE DONE.

BUT WHEN YOU TAKE FROM THEM CONTROL,
THEN COMES THE GOVERNMENT DOLE—
THE IRON RICE BOWL—
THE WELFARE ROLE—
THE CRADLE-TO-GRAVE GOAL.

HUMANS BECOME CLONES OF DRONES,
CONTROLLED AND TOLD
HOW TO LIVE WITHOUT GOALS;

Governed by the dominion elite,
Who see incentive as a goal to defeat,
So they can hold and control
The subservient soul.

They know well that independence
Threatens their power to control.

Still, in spite of oppression's ways
The spirit of independence stays.

It may be temporarily subdued,
But never, never removed.

For the spark of independence glows
In the heart of everyone,
Waiting to be fanned by the winds of demand,
Whenever freedom is found in the land.

It Might Have Been

IF WE COULD SEE DOWN THE CORRIDORS OF TIME
AHEAD OF THE PASSAGE THAT EXPERIENCE DEFINES,
OR GO BACK TO WHERE WE BEGAN,
AND START ALL OVER AGAIN
WITH THE KNOWLEDGE OF THE FUTURE WITHIN,
AND THE DREAMS OF WHAT MIGHT-HAVE-BEEN,

HOW MUCH DIFFERENT WOULD OUR TIME HERE BE?
HOW MANY FEWER MISTAKES WOULD WE SEE?

BUT HOW MUCH LESS WOULD WE KNOW
OF THE PERSON WITHIN OUR SOUL?

IF WE HARBOR REGRETS OF THE PAST,
AND STIR THEM CONTINUALLY IN MEMORY'S FLASK,
WE'LL ONLY SLIP FURTHER
DOWN DESPERATION'S PATH.

IT'S IMPOSSIBLE TO ERASE OUR IMPRINTS IN TIME,
OR THE MEMORIES THEY ENTWINE.

BUT WE CAN START FROM WHERE WE ARE
WITH THE EXPERIENCES WE'VE GAINED THUS FAR.

AND MAYBE WE SHOULD REVIEW AGAIN
THE TRAILS LAID DOWN BY THOSE WHO HAVE BEEN.

THEN, AS WE REMINISCE IN A FUTURE TIME,
AND THE PAST RUSHES BY
IN THE RECOLLECTIONS OF OUR MIND,
WE'LL NOT DESPAIR THE "MIGHT-HAVE-BEENS"
BY PREVENTING THEM FROM HAPPENING AGAIN.

It Takes Time

I WATCHED THE GARDEN GROW IN SUMMERTIME,
THE FRUIT AND SQUASH UPON THE VINE.

FROM SEED TO FULL-GROWN SQUASH
TOOK ONLY DAYS, UNTIL THE FROST.

I WATCHED FOR YEARS THE MIGHTY OAK
SO SLOWLY GROW, AS RINGS IT WROTE;

IT BORE THE ELEMENTS OF TIME
AS TO GREATER HEIGHTS IT CLIMBED.

THE SQUASH RIPENED IN DAYS SO FEW,
BUT IT WAS THE MIGHTY OAK WE KNEW.

AND WHAT OF YOU?
THE SQUASH—
OR THE MIGHTY OAK PURSUE?

Leaning against the Wind

LEANING AGAINST THE WIND'S
RELENTLESS DIN
BUILDS THE STRENGTH TO WIN.

WE CAN STAND AND FIGHT
OR CRUMBLE IN.

IT'S UP TO US
WHETHER WE LOSE OR WIN.

Love's Emotion

LOVE IS AN EMOTION OF FIDELITY AND TRUST.
IT EXPERIENCES A MAJESTY
FAR BEYOND THIS MORTAL DUST.

ITS ATTACHMENTS REACH ENDLESSLY,
AND CAN STIR ITS OPPOSITE VIEWS:
SELFISHNESS, HATE, AND REVENGE.
FORGIVENESS, TOO, TRAVELS THROUGH.

LOVE IS FOUND WITHIN THE RESTRAINTS
OF DUTY, SACRIFICE, AND LOYALTY.
VIRTUE AND DEVOTION PERVADE ITS DREAM.

LOVE IS THE PHYSICAL SHARING OF THE INFINITE.
IT ALLOWS US TO FEEL
THE IMMORTAL MAJESTY OF THE UNSEEN.
IT ECHOES A FOREVER THEME.

Love's Fire

LIKE THE BLAZING EARLY-MORNING SUN,
LOVE'S FIRE IS BEGUN.

WITH WARMING COMFORT AND DISGUISE
IT GREETS THE MORNING SKIES.

AS IT STIRS UNCERTAINTY ABOUT,
IT MIXES TURBULENCE
WITH RAINBOWS AND DROUGHT.

BUT AS IT PASSES TOWARD
ITS SUNSET HUES AND MATURING VIEWS,
ITS GENTLENESS RENEWS,

THEN SETS ON MORTAL SIGHT,
WARMING ELSEWHERE'S MORNING LIGHT.

Love's Hidden Treasures

THE WEARINESS OF DAILY LIFE
LAYS ITS COVERING OVER LOVE'S ROMANTICISM,
CONFUSING DUTY'S ENDLESS AFFECTION.

STILL, BENEATH
ITS LOYALTY AND DEVOTION ARE FORGING BONDS,
PREPARING FOR ANOTHER DAWN,
WHERE ITS TREASURES
WILL OPEN THEIR BEAUTY AGAIN
AND BEGIN TO CHURN EMOTIONS WITHIN.

THE TEDIUM OF DAILY LIFE
HOLDS WITHIN ITS SPELL,
THE SYNERGISM WHERE TRUE LOVE DWELLS.

Love's Silent Sounds

LOVE RINGS WITH MUTUALLY INDESCRIBABLE SOUNDS
THAT REACH BEYOND WORDS' EXPRESSIONS
AND ENCIRCLE US AROUND.

A MOTHER'S UNSPEAKABLE ATTACHMENT TO HER CHILD—
THE LONG COMPANIONSHIP THAT FIDELITY ALLOWS—

THE QUIET GOOD-BYES
AS LOVED ONES CLOSE THEIR EYES—

LASTING FRIENDSHIPS—
THE DEEP APPRECIATION FOR GOODNESS—

ALL FLOW FROM THE LANGUAGE OF THE SOUL,
AND ARE HINTS OF SOUNDS
BEYOND WHAT MORTALS KNOW.

FOR THESE BRIEF MOMENTS
WE ESCAPE OUR EARTHLY CONFINEMENTS
AND ARE CARRIED UPWARD,
AS WE SOAR UPON SERAPHIC WINGS
INTO THE REALMS OF THE UNSEEN.

Memories

Memories flood over us as we stroll among the quiet resting places of those we once knew.

I WANDERED THROUGH A QUIET PLACE
WHERE THE FLOWERS AND THE GRASS
BORE SOUNDS OF THE PAST
FROM THOSE WHO HAD GONE BEFORE.

WHERE THE WIND WHISPERED TO THE LISTENING EAR
FAMILIAR WORDS FROM THOSE ONCE NEAR.

THERE WERE HINTS IN THE ECHO SOUNDS
OF COURAGE AND HOPE FROM THOSE ONCE AROUND.

AND THE QUIETNESS WHERE I STROLLED
SPOKE PEACE TO MY YEARNING SOUL,
AND GAVE MORE MEANING TO MY EARTHLY GOALS.

THE MEMORIES AND LONGINGS
PUSHED ME ALONG
AS THE WIND-BLOWN FLOWERS WAVED ME ON.

Millstone

When sophistic thought
Feeds upon the innocent mind
And inherent faith is undermined—

When simple knowing
Is heaped with conjecture's doubt
And left to wander the faithless drought—

The fraud thus spawned
Stirs false hopelessness along
With all its hedonistic wrongs.

What sadness as truth recedes
To the pedagogic seeds.

Better to drown in the waters deep
Than to offend innocent belief.[25]

The Moment

Each moment we live may seem
An unimportant dream
As it passes along life's busy stream.

Yet together, these moments we weave
Form the tapestry of the history we leave.

They stand forever in the annals of time
Indelibly inscribed in the immortal mind.

Though instant in the spectrum of time,
They are imprints of a permanent kind,
And speak together of the person we'll find.

So, as we live our moments today,
We must measure them well
For what they will tell;
Moment by moment we excel.
Moment by moment we descend as well.

Mortality's Time

When we examine our fragile existence,
With life's uncertainties, wars, and pestilence,
We wonder, sometimes with fear,
How long we might be here.

Is there further purpose?
Or is life only a pantomime—
An accident in time?

When our course here is run,
Is life forever done?

Or is there meaning to our being here?
Are there unseen hosts helping—caring—near?

When we consider life's complexities,
The wonder of our birth,
Thought, reason, and human worth,
Rationalism speaks of a far-more complex plan
Than an accidental existence on earth.

And if our being might be planned,
Was our time here determined beforehand?

Are we directed and protected along the way,
To insure our appointed stay?

WE QUESTION THE WARS, DISEASES,
UNTIMELY DEATHS THAT COME OUR WAY,
CHILD MORTALITY,
ALL THE TRAGEDIES LIFE DISPLAYS,
THE ANOMALIES THAT ABOUND,
AND THE SADNESS WE HAVE FOUND.

BUT IF DEITY GOVERNS IN THE AFFAIRS OF MAN,
THERE MUST BE AN ETERNAL PLAN,
WITH JUSTICE, PROVISION, AND REASON,
BEFORE IT ALL BEGAN.

IF WE TRAVEL LIFE'S ROADS,
HELPING OTHERS CARRY THEIR LOADS,
BEING DECENT TO OUR FELLOW MAN,
BEING AS CAREFUL AS WE CAN——
WE SHOULD LIVE OUT OUR PLAN.

WE SHOULD NOT QUESTION OR FRET-OUT OUR DAYS,
OR WORRY HOW LONG OUR STAY.

JUST MOVE OUR SIGHTS FURTHER THAN WE SEE——
HAVE FAITH AND CERTAINTY
THAT WHAT WILL BE
WILL AGREE WITH ETERNITY'S THEOPHANY.

Mother

THE WARMTH OF THE SUN IN EARLY SPRING
IS THE FEELING MOTHERS BRING.

THE SUMMER COMES WITH GENTLE DAYS
AND MOTHER'S WAYS.

THE SMELL OF LEAVES, AS FALL COMES BY,
THE HARVEST AND THE CLEAR, CRISP SKY,
REMIND US MOTHER IS NIGH.

DURING WINTER WINDS, COLD AND NUMB,
ALWAYS HOME TO MOTHER WE COME.

AFTER WINTER'S REST, AGAIN THERE IS SPRING,
WITH LIFE IT TEEMS, AS ALSO MOTHERS BRING.

THE SEASONS' WONDROUS TIMES
RHYME WITH MOTHER'S KIND.

Musical Classics

The golden tones
Of musical classics,
That fill symphonic air,
Converge
With their likeness elsewhere—

Entwining in harmony
The mortal sphere
With sounds of cosmic peers—

And bring—ever-clearer,
The infinite reaches—ever-nearer.

My Sunshine

A tribute to our daughter Andrea, who died of cancer in the springtime, just before her fifth birthday.

Little daughter of mine,
Who lived here such a brief time,

Best friend you were
To your mother and me,
And the family.

Your beautiful red hair,
Your spirit so fair,
With so little time to spare.

Your gentle ways,
Though short your days,
Filled our lives with sunshine's rays.

Why, so often asked, so often cried,
Must long your presence be denied?

Why must such innocence leave?
Why this cause to grieve?

We thought your days so few,
But who can judge eternal views.

You accomplished more in your short stay,
More love, than most in years display.

Your memory binds us to your soul
And bears us upward toward eternal goals.

You've deepened our faith
And helped wash away
The sophistry of our day,
And lifted us to a time far more sublime.

Thank you, my little sunshine.

Names

WHEN FIRST WE HEAR NEW NAMES,
AND AS THEY BECOME MORE FAMILIAR SOUNDS,
WE WONDER—
WHOSE FACES DO THEY CLAIM, THESE NAMES?
SO WE SEARCH THE CROWDS AROUND.

TO KNOW SUCH PEOPLE AND THEIR NAMES
ADDS MEANING TO OUR OWN, AND FAME;

A LITTLE OF WHAT THEY ARE
BECOMES A PART OF US
AND INFLUENCES THE THINGS WE DO.

BUT IT'S EVEN MORE IMPORTANT WHEN
THEY KNOW OUR NAME AND SPEAK IT NOW AND THEN.

A NOD FROM THE CROWD, A SMILE,
MAKES US FEEL MORE WORTHWHILE.

SUCH PEOPLE WE ALL SHOULD BE,
CHARISMATIC, SUCCESSFUL, YET NOT TOO PROUD
TO INCLUDE OTHERS IN OUR CROWD.

Never Alone

WHENEVER UPON THE LONELY SEA
AND THE TIDES OF DECISION
SEEM PULLING THEE
ALONG THE WAVES
WHERE YOU DON'T WANT TO BE;

KNOW THE SEAS WILL CALM
AND THE TIDES SUBSIDE,
AND YOU'LL BE STRONGER
FOR HAVING TRIED,
AND READY—MORE READY,
FOR THE NEXT HIGH TIDE.

AND YOU'LL KNOW—YOU'LL KNOW—
I'LL BE HELPING YOU ROW!

The Nuclear Family

THE NUCLEAR FAMILY IMPLIES
COHESION AND POWER FROM INSIDE;

MOTHER AND FATHER, COMBINED
WITH CHILDREN CIRCLING ENTWINED;

HELD TOGETHER BY UNYIELDING LAWS,
WITH FAITHFUL CONDUCT AND A DETERMINED CAUSE.

BUT BURST THIS NUCLEUS BY THE INFUSION
OF BROKEN TRUST,
THEN RAGING STORMS,
IN EXPONENTIAL FORM,
CRUSH THE TIMELESS NORM,
AND BARREN ECHOES ARE SOON TO MOURN.

Ocean Tales

What of the moon-pulled ocean swells?
If they could speak, what tales they'd tell
Of heroes caught in their throws,
And the life and death they know.

And the ocean deep—
How many dreams has she put to sleep?
How many has she helped to keep?

In her raging storms forlorn—
In her fogs, and warning horns—
How many from their moorings torn?

Listen to the ocean rolls,
The hush of her tidal flows,
And life as it goes.

Old Memories

That old barn,
Weather-worn,
Wind-shorn, and torn—

Echoing a time long past
Of work and life therein.

And the old fence with rails broken-in—
Moss-covered, grayed, and dim,
Recalling times where memories begin—

And mementos aforetime
That remind the mind—
The pictures and letters,
Old stories and rhyme—

What do they hold,
These relics of old?
What memories untold
As they stir through the past,
With sunshine and shadows cast.

LBLEE
93

Olden Ones

*Dedicated to my mother, who spent the last few
months of her life in a nursing home.*

Quietly they dined, these olden ones,
With so few words their morsels ate,
Their time grown late.

I wondered what thoughts
With quietude they shield,
As pensive wrought
Their memories near-stilled,
Yet, forgotten not.

The wisdom beneath their silver hair,
What experiences to share!

Still, quietly they're there,
With few who care,
These olden, golden ones,
Their time near-done,
Patiently awaiting what next will come.

Opposition

ONLY FROM OPPOSITION'S VIEW
CAN KNOWLEDGE BE PURSUED.

HOW CAN WE KNOW SUCCESS
WITHOUT SOME FAILURE TO TEST?
OR KNOW THE GOOD WITHOUT THE BAD?
OR HAPPINESS WITHOUT THE SAD?

JOY IS IMPOSSIBLE TO UNDERSTAND
UNTIL WE HAVE MET SORROW FIRST-HAND.

HEALTH, PLENTY, AND WARMTH ARE ONLY WORDS
UNTIL THEIR OPPOSITES HAVE OCCURRED.

WITHOUT THE LOSING PACE,
NO ONE CAN WIN THE RACE.

THESE ARE THE REASONS FOR MORTALITY'S STAY;
COMPREHENSION COMES IN NO OTHER WAY.

THIS IS THE FRUIT OF EDEN-TIME
THAT HAS BROUGHT KNOWLEDGE TO MANKIND.

OUR LIFE HERE WAS NEVER MEANT TO BE
A UTOPIAN SPREE WITHOUT ADVERSITY.

OUR REST COMES AFTER THE TRIALS ARE DONE—
NOT WHILE THE RACE IS BEING RUN.

Overcoming

Whenever I'm tempted to go away
From the rules and conduct I should obey,
I turn to the music of the classics
Instead of the songs of the day.

I read the words of inspired books,
And at my commitments look.

To the good and decent I open my mind
To see what I can find.

I write my thoughts, my philosophies,
And all that I do—
And poetry, too.

And In silent reverie I remember my friends
And loved ones who were close to me—
Those who have entered immortality.

I measure my life against the good I see
In my friends, family,
And those who are heroes to me.

I remember, too,
That others are watching the things I do.

BY KEEPING MY MIND ON THESE THINGS,
AND LESS ON WHAT THE WORLD BRINGS,
I'M ABLE TO TRAVEL DOWN LIFE'S BUSY ROAD
WITH A MUCH-LESS TROUBLING LOAD.

AND WHEN THE END OF MY LIFE HERE
DRAWS NEAR,
AND MY LOOK INTO ETERNITY BEGINS TO CLEAR,
I KNOW I'LL HAVE NOTHING TO FEAR.

Peace

Whenever our conduct slips downward
From the level of our ideals,
Our minds become troubled
With the burdens we feel.

Some say, "The troubled feeling will go
If we lower our values to our conduct below.

"Discount," they say, "old rules of the past—
Ideals never really last;
They change, as the winds,
To what anyone thinks.
It's foolish to hold to the notions of old—
Go along with the thoughts of the day
And forget what traditions say."

Yet deep within the still-troubled mind,
There is a lingering, haunting doubt
Where peace is hard to find.

Have the traditions of the past slipped away
As some people say?
Is there any peace
In the drifting, shifting ideals of the day?

If so, why are we still troubled
As we live below the ideals we know?

The laws, the rules, the conduct of old,
The values of decency
And goodness they hold
Are not easily lost, as we're often told.

They stand as sentinels, an invincible sign,
A guide for all mankind;
And whenever discarded,
The deluded will find
A deeply troubled and unhappy mind;
And nations will disappear
In the annals of time.

The only way to find peace that lasts
Is to move our actions above our mistakes,
And hold to the traditions of the past.

Peaceful Dawn

A PEACEFUL CALM
SILKENS EARTHEN DAWN
AS ITS EARLY MORNING
SHADES ARE DRAWN;

A MELODIOUS MIRACLE
WITH ITS SOUNDS AND SONGS.

FROM THE FIELDS AND HILLS
FLOWERS OPEN THEIR NECTAR-FILLS
AND LEAVES DRAW IN THEIR NEEDS.

EVERYWHERE
ACROSS THE THREADS OF DAWN
AN AWAKENING CREEPS ALONG—
AND WE FEEL THE WONDER
OF WHERE WE BELONG.

The Person Within

It's easy enough to appear in control
When there are no challenges to know.

It's easy enough to deceive the crowd
When there are no darkening clouds.

It's easy to appear strong
When pushed along
With no obstacles or wrongs,
Or never to worry or fret
When all of your needs are easily met.

Or when the road is smooth
And the wind is at your back,
It's easy to put on an act.

But when stress and challenges arise,
And despair and confusion cloud your eyes,
When nothing goes right and you must fight,
Your true character comes to light.

You can no longer hide the person inside
When the pressure is on and rough's the ride.

Your true measure is drawn,
As the struggles go on.

Until you have experienced
The challenges of life,
And shown how well you can fight,
You'll never know the person within,
Or what you are really like.

Propensities

As the mystery of our propensities
Becomes clear,
Should their inclinations be feared?

What of the ideas and ideals we embrace?
Why the natural attractions
Of the human race?

Why do they haunt us so,
These inclinations entwined with soul?

How far back do they go,
These propensities we know?

Of those we claim our own,
To what are they most likely prone?

Those of a kind that nurture and refine,
Or those to which defilement align?

Do our propensities reveal our soul,
And what we know,
And where we'll go?

Do they control
How through life we'll stroll?

I'm afraid so.

Reaper

Life's winter comes by
As time seems quietly done,
And the reaper comes—
Grim to some—
And ushers in seeming oblivion.

But as the morning sun
Faithfully brightens horizon's rim,
Again and again,
Dispelling the darkness within,

So the reaper's harvest—
Of old, and young, and everyone—
Speaks of morning to come,
And gathers, only to shine
Among cosmic suns,

To open eyes we thought at rest
To conscious everlastingness.

Responsibility

We are responsible, each one,
For the deeds we've done,
The mistakes that come,
And the accolades won.

Each action becomes a part of our soul,
Our mind, our whole—
That which we know.

The soul can grow, or crumble so,
Depending on what we know.

We can't shift blame,
Take false claim,
Hide from shame,
Or diminish our fame.

We're never so alone or on our own,
As for what we've grown
From the seeds we've sown.

Rest

There is a dream, in the heart of everyone,
Of a place to retreat when the work is done;

Somewhere to go where a stillness is in the air,
And a quietness there;

Where gentler sounds are around,
And solitude and healing found;

Where there is a simpleness in things,
And the rest a slower pace brings.

Somewhere to be alone—
In a mountain home,
Or near ocean waves,
Or a quiet desert cave,
Or a home, or an apartment
Near the busy city markets.

Somewhere, where the pace stops
Or slowly winds down,
Away from the rushing, hustling
Crowds of the town.

Somewhere where we can gather our thoughts,
Untie the knots that are often caught
As we weave our way
Through the tapestry of the day.

There needs to be a refuge—somewhere—
For everyone, when the work is done.

Restraints

I HEAR A MOURNFUL CRY
IN AMORALITY'S DELUSIVE WIND,
AN EMPTY, HOLLOW SOUND
BLOWING ACROSS ITS HEAPS OF WHIMS.

I HEAR A STUMBLING, DRIFTING,
RECKLESS RUMBLING THEREIN,
DRIVEN BY NIHILISM'S HEDONISTIC DIN
WHERE OBLIVION'S DESPERATION RUSHES IN.

THE VULTURES CIRCLE OVERHEAD
PATIENTLY WAITING,
WAITING FOR THEIR FAITHLESS DEAD.

I HEAR A DESPERATE PLEADING,
GRAPPLING, GROPING;
SEARCHING FOR PURPOSE, FOR HOPE,
FOR CONSTRAINTS TO LIVE WITHIN.

I HEAR A CRY TO FLEE THE FAITHLESS DROUGHT;
A CRY TO WREST THE WRETCHED GHOST
OF WANTON HOSTS OUT.

I HEAR A CRY TO OPEN THE RIDGED GATES
OF DUTY, LOYALTY, AND TRUST'S CONSTRAINTS;
A CRY FOR MORAL STRENGTH.

I HEAR A CRY FOR FREEDOM'S RESTRAINTS. [26]

179

Revenge

Revenge withers the soul
"Like an uprooted weed
Wilting in the sun."[27]

Such is the consuming fire
Of the revengeful one.

Peace flees, forever gone,
As long as vengeance hisses on.

Stooped under its burden,
Injuring mostly those from whom it flows,
As they conjure the barren past.

Only forgiveness can quench
This venomous wrath.

The River of Life

For ages the river runs—
Forever—never done.

Its soul rushes over rocks,
Down falls,
Through canyon walls.

Memories whisper along the way,
As we listen to what they say.

Some troubled waters it knows;
Some lost in its undertow.

During gentler flows,
Its water, low and slow,
Speaks peace to the weary souls.

Life goes as the river flows,
Forever learning as we go;

Carving our place,
Experiencing the race,
As challenges we face
At the river's pace.

Robin

As the robin brings-in early spring,
She personifies continuing life
In her maternal wings.

I watched as she built her nest,
As she plied her skills
For her future guests.

I wondered, a silent part,
Where she had learned
So precise an art.

Soon appeared small eggs,
Protected and warmed
By her nesting ways.

It seemed only days
Before life's cycle displayed.

I watched as she cared for her brood;
So quickly they feathered and grew;
So soon they flew.

Her nest empty now,
The summer bowed.
Soon winter, then spring
And the red-breasted fowl.

The Shift of the Sails

When we are young, our hopes
Run with the wide-open seas;
Our goal is the daily catch
And the excitement we see.

But as age pushes us along,
We change our sails to where they belong.
We shift from the drift
And steer for the distant shores.

The sooner we set our sails
For those distant shores,
The less troubling will be
The challenges in store,
And the safer we'll finish the race.

Those who set their sails
With the hope that the sea
Is larger, more distant than it seems to be,
Will find those shores afar,
Just as they really are.

The distant sea,
The horizons to be,
Soon become reality.

Society's Ruse

PHILOSOPHERS, SINCE TIME BEGAN,
HAVE TRIED TO LEAD US TO THE PROMISED LAND.

IN THEIR INTELLECTUAL PIETY,
THEY HAVE SOUGHT THE PERFECT SOCIETY.

YET WHENEVER THEIR IDEAS THEY'VE TRIED,
MANKIND HAS SUFFERED AND DIED.

WHY, IN ALL THEIR SPURIOUS WISDOM,
COULD THEY NOT FIND
THE PERFECT SOCIETY FOR MANKIND?

BECAUSE THEIR EARTH-BOUND MINDS
WON'T LET THEM SEARCH
BEYOND THEIR KNOWN CONFINES.

FOR THE ANSWERS COME OF OLD,
AS ANCIENTS TOLD,
FROM SINAI'S ABODE.

FROM LAWS ON STONE, DIVINELY SHOWN,
OF PROVEN RULES WE ALL HAVE KNOWN
THAT ECHO BACK BEFORE EARTH'S BEGINNING TIME,
REFLECTING COSMOS' PARADIGM.

RULES THAT PRESERVE
ALL WHO OBSERVE.

YET, THE SHIFTING PHILOSOPHIES
OF SOPHISTIC SWAY
MORE EASILY ENWRAP OUR CARNAL WAY,
THOUGH THE TRAGEDIES OF THEIR CRIMES
ARE SCATTERED UPON THE SANDS OF TIME—
HIDDEN MYSTERIES OF SOCIAL DECLINE.

WHILE ALL THAT WAS NEEDED TO PRESERVE MANKIND
WAS INSCRIBED UPON STONES IN OLDEN TIME.

STILL—WE STEAL, AND LIE,
DEITY'S NAME PROFANE.
WE TAKE A LIFE, OR SOMEONE ELSE'S WIFE.

WE COVET WHAT OTHERS HAVE,
WORSHIP NOT, NOR PRAY,
NOR KEEP A SACRED DAY.

WE IGNORE WHAT PARENTS SAY,
AND CREATION'S POWER BETRAY.

WE HONOR THE PHILOSOPHIES OF OUR DAY
AND THROW THE STONES OF SINAI AWAY.

Sounds

THERE ARE MANY SOUNDS AROUND—
SOUNDS FROM NATURE'S WONDERS,
AND MIGHTY THUNDERS;
SOUNDS OF MOUNTAIN STREAMS AND ROLLING SEAS;
THE WIND AND RUSTLING LEAVES;

THE ANIMALS, BIRDS, AND CREATURES ALL,
RESPONDING TO NATURE'S CALL;

MUSIC THAT FILLS THE AIR,
RESOUNDS FROM EVERYWHERE.

BUT SOUNDS MOST LASTING,
MOST TREASURED, AND REMEMBERED
ARE SOUNDS OF SHARING,
OF LOVED-ONES CARING—

"I NEED YOU," FROM A CHILD;
"HELP ME PLEASE, FOR A WHILE;"

TRUSTING SOUNDS OF "I'LL BE THERE,"
"I LOVE YOU,"
"I KNOW YOU CARE;"

SOUNDS OF SIMPLE PLEAS TO BE NEAR,
TO CALM SOMEONE'S FEAR;

Of short good-byes, lonely cries,
And silent sounds from loving eyes;

Forgiving words we've heard;

Sounds of deep respect;
Of friendships met and kept;
And final good-byes
As life closes its eyes—

These are the sounds that time enshrines!
These are the sounds that love entwines!

Stress

To stress:

"Tormenter of my soul,
I care little for what you know.
I seek a life with no worries,
Problems, failures, or challenges to grow.

"To lie peacefully upon sunny shores,
With nothing to resist anymore,
Is the life I'm looking for."

Stresses' answer:

"My presence will support you in the end;
Come along and you'll find me a friend.

"I generate the adrenalin within
That inspires winners to win;
I'm the catalyst
That brings extra courage to men.

"I'm the place where strength is tested;
In me the magnificence of creation is vested.

"Duty and loyalty with me abide;
Upon responsibility's wings I ride.

"Ideas, risk, and uncertainty come along too,
Which brings out
The individual ruggedness in you.

"The defenders of the free,
The mighty comrades in arms depend on me.

"I'm that which moves history along;
I ride the crest of adventure's brawn.

"Learn to greet me at your door
As friend and mentor.

"Become acquainted with my ways,
And draw strength during my stays.

"Wait awhile before judging
And you will see,
You'll become better because of me.

"Having persevered,
You will have conquered
Whom at first you feared."

Struggles' Virtue

How many have risen to heights renowned
From the lowliest situations around?

How many have climbed to the top
By their own effort and thought?

How many, with no beauty to embrace,
Have reached prominence
With refinement and grace,
While others were born
With opulence, wealth,
Natural beauty, and good health?

There seems to be imbalance at life's door.
But, who would you choose as your mentor
To teach you the lessons of life?
Or how to survive amid trouble and strife?
Or when lost in a storm on raging seas?

One who had no obstacles to overcome,
Or one who had fought and won?

Thunderous Sky

With the sun in the early morn
Comes the hope of new-life born.

All creation comes alive
As nature opens her eyes.

Little trouble is seen
As the early sunbeams shine on everything.

Soon, though, the clouds begin to appear,
Casting shadows, shade, and darkening fear.

As thunderous night
Creeps across noonday light,
Nature bows and hides,
Tranquility goes, the wind blows,
The rain comes and the torrents flow,
The lightning glows.

But when the sun sets,
And nature greets its midnight guests,
Life's sleeping soul calms and rests,
And quietly waits until the next day breaks.

What comes from the sun, the rain,
And nature's strains and pains?

THE GROWTH WE KNOW,
THE MOUNTAIN SNOW,
LAKES AND STREAMS,
AND THE LIFE THEY BRING—
WHICH OTHERWISE WOULD DIE.

THUNDEROUS SKY, PLEASE ROLL BY.

Time

Time moves along, in the immensity of space,
Carving out the history of the human race;

And echoes, as it moves along,
Its warnings to the traveling throngs.

Its pendulum sweeps with precision and grace,
Never looking back or slackening its pace.

Each traveler leaves his mark in time
To help or deter those following behind.

As sorrow comes our way
Time guarantees it will not stay;

Just as happiness can never be sure
To always grace our door.

All things, someday,
Given enough time, will pass away.

It takes time to achieve,
Time to believe, and to learn,
And in time we leave.

A Time to Come

THERE IS A TIME TO COME
WHEN THIS LIFE IS DONE,
WHEN LOVED ONES MEET,
AND FRIENDS AND PEOPLE GREET.

WHEN THAT TIME COMES
WE WILL LEARN THAT LIFE FOREVER RUNS.

EVEN THE DOUBTING SOUL MUST GO;
EVEN THE ATHEIST WILL KNOW;

AND THE MURDERERS AND CHEATS
CANNOT RETREAT;
THEIR VICTIMS THEY MUST MEET.

WHAT SORROW FOR SOME
WHEN THEY COME.

WE CAN DENY, DISCLAIM, AND IGNORE,
BUT LIFE FOREVER MORE
WILL REVEAL ITSELF AT DEATH'S DOOR.

SO LIVE YOUR EARTH-BOUND DAYS
KNOWING THE FUTURE UPON YOU LAYS.

THEN YOU WILL GREET WITH PEACE
THE DEEDS YOU'VE DONE,
WHEN YOUR TIME HAS COME.

Try

I WATCHED THE CLOUDS DRIFT LEISURELY BY
AS THE SUMMER SUN WARMED THE SKY.

CONTENTEDLY
THEY PASSED OVER ME.

AS THE AFTERNOON BREEZE CAME BY,
THEY BEGAN TO BUILD UP HIGH.

I WATCHED AS THEY CHURNED
IN THE DARKENING SKY.

WHAT POWER AND FORCE
IN THEIR TURBULENT COURSE!

HOW THE THUNDER SOUNDED
AND THE LIGHTNING BLAZED!
HOW LIKE THE BUILDERS AND WINNERS
THEY PLAYED!

HOW WE ALL MUST BREAK FROM OUR REST,
AND CHURN IN AN UNKNOWN QUEST
TO BECOME OUR BEST!

Unshackled

THE WISE PERSON UNSHACKLES THE IRON WEIGHTS
OF MEMORY'S HOARDED TREASURES OF MISCONDUCT,
SETS ASIDE MISTAKES, CORRECTS ERRORS,
AND IDENTIFIES RIGHT AND WRONG;
THEN TRAVELS EVER ONWARD AND UPWARD
ALONG THE PATH OF MORAL VALUES;

EVER MORE SENSITIVE
TO NATURE'S GIFTS AND SOUNDS,
EVER MORE SENSITIVE TO GOODNESS,
EVER MORE AT PEACE,
EVER MORE FREE.

The Winds of Adversity

Suffering is the teacher of the soul and allows us to understand joy.

FROM LIFE'S MOUNTAINS AND VALLEYS
AND UNKNOWN SEAS
BLOW THE WINDS OF ADVERSITY.

AT FIRST WE SHUN THE FORCEFUL THRUSTS
THESE WINDS BLOW UPON US.
BUT AS WE REACH OUR GOALS,
WE BECOME EQUAL TO THE BLOWS.

THEN WE LOOK BACK WITH PITY ON THOSE
WHO TRAVEL THEIR COURSE
WITH NO WINDS A-BLOW—
NO FALLINGS TO ARISE—
OR SAND, OR TEARS IN THEIR EYES.

OUR SUFFERING, THE LEARNING STUFF,
NOW FEELS GOOD TO US.

OH SUFFERING, INSCRIBER OF THE SOUL,
GLORY TO THE WINDS, THE WINDS THAT BLOW.

Woman

Written to my wife, Cleo, on Mothers' Day 1995.

BEFORE THE SUN STIRS ITS YELLOW HAZE
AROUND COURTYARDS, THROUGH WINDOWS,
OR UPON OUR WAKENING GAZE;

BEFORE THE BIRDS SING IN EARLY DAWN
OR THE NIGHT IS FULLY GONE
YOU CAN HEAR HER FOOTSTEPS' SOUND,
FEEL HER WARM, WORN GOWN
AS SHE MAKES HER MATERNAL ROUNDS.

A GENTLE REFINEMENT SETTLES IN HER PATH
AS SHE TOILS ABOUT HER TASKS.

HER VELVET TOUCH IS PRIZED MORE THAN GOLD.
HER MOVEMENTS—A MELODIOUS ODE.

WHEN TROUBLE AND SORROW
DESCEND UPON HER CROWD,
SHE WEAVES HER WEB, A PROTECTIVE SHROUD,
DISPELLING DARKENED CLOUDS.

SHE ENDOWS HER IMMORTAL IMPRINT
WITH DIGNITY AND GRACE
AS SHE GOES ABOUT
PRESERVING THE HUMAN RACE.

A Woman's Hands

Nothing equals a woman's touch.

A WOMAN'S HANDS—SO LOYAL,
WORN AND WRINKLED FROM HER TOIL—

HELPING SO OFTEN OTHERS' NEEDS—
GENTLY TOUCHING, CARESSING—
WITH WARMTH BEQUEATH.

HER HANDS CRADLE WARM GOOD-BYES—
CARRYING—LOVING—COMFORTING CRIES.

THOUGH YOUNG OR OLD
HER HANDS UNFOLD—
HER WORLD TO UPHOLD.

Research Notes and Comments

These notes and comments are not extensive and come from only a few sources. These sources are, however, scholarly and well-documented, and deserve a thorough study. They are included to lend credibility to the statements in *Cosmic Whispers*.

There are, undoubtably, statements or parts of statements that originate from what others have written or said that have become part of my own thinking. Seldom are ideas totally original. I have tried, however, to give credit wherever possible.

1. Michael Denton, *Evolution: A Theory In Crisis* (Bethesda, Maryland: Adler & Adler, 1985), p. 69, gives insight into the reasons that the seventeenth- and eighteenth-century explanations for physical phenomenon were moving away from the traditional Biblical accounts.

2. Denton, *Evolution: A Theory In Crisis*, p. 67.

3. Denton, *Evolution: A Theory In Crisis*, p. 75, quotes the following from a statement made by Julian Huxley at a conference in 1959: "The first point to make about Darwin's *theory* is that it is no longer a *theory* but *fact*...Darwinism has come of age so to speak. We are no longer having to bother about establishing the *fact* of evolution... [*emphasis added*]"

Philip E. Johnson, *Darwin On Trial* (Washington, D.C.: Regnery Gateway, 1991), p. 130. Johnson quotes the following statement of Pierre Teihard de Chardin: "Is evolution a theory, a system, or a hypothesis? It is much more—it is a general postulate to which all theories, all hypotheses, all systems must henceforth bow and which they must satisfy in order to be thinkable and true. Evolution is a light which illuminates all facts, a trajectory which all lines of thought must follow—this is what evolution is."

Henry M. Morris, *The Long War Against God* (Grand Rapids, Michigan: Baker Book House, 1989), p. 24. The following is a statement by geneticist Richard Goldschmidt: "Evolution of the animal and plant world is considered by all those entitled to judgment to be a fact for which no further proof is needed. But in spite of nearly a century of work and discussion there is still no unanimity in regard to the details of the means of evolution."

The above quotes are examples of the impregnable evolutionary dogmatism prevalent in much of the scientific community, all of which are antithetical to the search for truth.

4. Alexander Solzhenitsyn, *Warning To The West* (New York: The Noonday Press, 1976), p. 127.

For further information on the amoral and philosophical impact that Darwinian Evolution, atheism, and its attending nihilism has had on humanity, I recommend the following studies: Phillip E. Johnson, *Reason in the Balance* (Downers Grove, Illinois: InterVarsity Press, 1995); Erik von Kuehnelt-Leddihn, *Leftism Revisited* (Washington, D.C.: Regnery Gateway, 1990); Robert H. Bork, *Slouching Towards Gomorrah* (New York: Regan Books, 1996).

5. A few of the well-documented, scholarly arguments that identify evolution's weaknesses, uncertainties, and missing links can be found in the following publications: Johnson, *Darwin on Trial*; Johnson, *Reason in the Balance*; Denton, *Evolution: A Theory In Crisis*; Morris, *The Long War Against God*; David Foster, *The Philosophical Scientists* (New York: Dorset Press, 1985); Michael J. Behe, *Darwin's Black Box* (New York: The Free Press, 1996).

6. Johnson, *Darwin On Trial*, pp. 46-47. Darwin conceded that the state of the fossil evidence was "the most obvious and gravest objection which can be argued against my theory."

Darwin also asked the question, "Why, if species have descended from other species by insensibly fine gradations, do we not everywhere see innumerable transitional forms? Why is not all nature in confusion instead of the species being, as we see them, well defined?"

He, of course, invented answers consistent with his theories, as do all evolutionary scientists.

7. Denton, *Evolution: A Theory In Crisis,* pp. 192-94. American paleontologists Miles Eldredge and Stephen Jay Gould, because of the lack of evidence in the fossil record for Darwinian gradualism, proposed a model of evolution known as "punctuated equilibrium, . . . an episodic process occurring in fits and starts interspaced with long periods of stasis". . . .

"The punctuational model of Eldridge and Gould has been widely publicized but, ironically, while the theory was developed specifically to account for the absence of transitional varieties between species, its major effect seems to have been to draw widespread attention to the gaps in the fossil record. When Eldridge raised the subject with a group of science writers a few years back his views were widely reported and even reached the front page of the British newspaper *The Guardian Weekly,* but it was the absence of the transitional forms which particularly caught the attention of the reporter. According to an article entitled 'Missing Believed Nonexistent':

" 'If life had evolved into its wondrous profusion of creatures little by little, then one would expect to find fossils of transitional creatures which were a bit like what went before them and a bit like what came after. But no one has yet found any evidence of such transitional creatures. This oddity has been attributed to gaps in the fossil record which gradualists expected to fill when rock strata of the proper age had been found. In the last decade, however, geologists have found rock layers of all divisions of the last 500 million years and no transitional forms were contained in them.' "

The fossil record is so troubling that paleontologists and scientists in related disciplines have found it necessary to invent alternate possible hypotheses to fill in the missing links of gradualism's improbability. Darwin himself acknowledged that "imagination must fill up the very wide blanks." (Denton, *Evolution: A Theory In Crisis,* p. 117.) In the field of evolution, scientific imagination runs rampant.

Johnson, *Darwin On Trial,* pp. 45-62; and Denton, *Evolution: A*

207

Theory In Crisis, pp.157-97. I recommend a thorough reading of these references in order to understand how troubling the fossil record—or lack of it—is to the Darwinian theory of gradualism in evolution.

8. Foster, pp. 68-79; Denton, *Evolution: A Theory in Crisis,* pp. 308-25; and Behe, *Darwin's Black Box.* These sources identify and explain the enormous complexity of molecular biology and the impossibility of chance directing such complexity.

9. Foster, p. 47. This reference documents Julian Huxley's statement when confronted with the mathematical improbability of any chance creation.

10. Denton, *Evolution: A Theory In Crisis,* pp. 249-73. This reference gives information on the unbridgeable division between life and inorganic nature.

11. Many of the micro-miniaturized machines in molecular biology are so small that they must be magnified a million times before they become visible to the human eye, and yet they are so sophisticated and specific in their function that anything man has created pales in comparison.

For information that challenges any attempt of science to use the molecular evidence in support of evolution, read: Johnson, *Darwin On Trial,* pp. 86-99; Foster, pp. 60-84; and Behe, *Darwin's Black Box.*

12. See note number 8 for information on the time it would take for chance to create anything meaningful. You will soon discover the meaning of never.

13. *Entropy:* Its meaning as used in *Cosmic Whispers* is best defined by its synonyms of inertness, formlessness, disorder, and uncertainty.

Random House Webster's College Dictionary (New York: Random House, 1996) defines entropy as "a state of disorder or

208

disorganization" (definition 4). *Webster's Ninth New Collegiate Dictionary* (Springfield, Massachusetts: Merriam Webster Inc., 1985), definition 3, says entropy is "the degradation of the matter and energy in the universe to an ultimate state of inert uniformity."

Foster, p. 37, defines entropy as "the measure of the improbability of entities being in one pre-decided state; it is the measure of uncertainty, the uncertainty of specificity."

14. Denton, *Evolution: A Theory In Crisis*, pp. 339-40. Comparing living things with mechanical or manmade creations: "One of the principal weaknesses of this argument was raised by David Hume, who pointed out that organisms may be only superficially like machines but natural in essence. Only if an object is strikingly analogous to a machine in a very profound sense would the inference to design be valid. Hume's criticism is generally considered to have fatally weakened the basic analogical assumptions upon which the inference to design is based, and it is certainly true that neither in the eighteenth century nor at any time during the past two centuries has there been sufficient evidence for believing that living organisms were like machines in any profound sense. . . .

"It has only been over the past twenty years with the molecular biological revolution and with the advances in cybernetic and computer technology that Hume's criticism has been finally invalidated and the analogy between organisms and machines has at last become convincing. . . .

"In the atomic fabric of life we have found a reflection of our own technology."

The Incredible Machine (Washington, D.C.: National Geographic Society, 1986). It is not uncommon today for scientists to refer to biological creations as similar to very complex machines. An example is this incredible pictorial study on the human body. See Also Behe, pp. 51-73.

Interestingly, I once asked an atheist to describe death. His reply: "Death is a mechanical failure." I do not ascribe to this definition or to the idea that biological life is merely an incredibly complicated machine. Biological life is complicated and wondrous, but it is alive because it is animated by infinitely finer organized matter.

15. *Specificity:* In *Cosmic Whispers*, specificity is used to describe the complex, specific organization and function of entities of molecular biology. The more complicated an organization, the greater its specificity.

In Foster, p. 39, specificity is defined as "the measure of the improbability of a pattern which actually occurs against a background of alternatives."

As an example, the molecule hemoglobin in humans is made of 574 specific positions of 20 amino acids. The possible alternative arrangements, or permutations, of these 574 amino acids is approximately 10^{650}, of which only one could be hemoglobin. (Foster, p. 80.) "The specificity of the hemoglobin protein is, [therefore,] represented by the number 10^{650}. What this means is that if hemoglobin evolved by chance, there would only be one chance in 10^{650} of it actually occurring . . . .

"These figures have to be set against the fact that the universe [according to science] is only 10^{18} seconds old, and so there is no possibility whatsoever of life having evolved through Darwin's theory of natural selection operating on chance mutations." (Foster, p. viii.)

Darwin totally underestimated the time his theory would need: "trillions of times longer than the existence of the universe," (Foster, p. 82) and then it would be impossible for chance to work such a miracle.

Foster, in summing up the enormous specificity in molecular biology, says "the specificities (improbabilities) involved in organic life are of incredible degree. Haemoglobin has an improbability of 10^{650} while the DNA of the T 4 bacteriophage has an improbability of $10^{78,000}$ . . . . The T 4 phage, [is] a tiny creature which preys upon bacteria: its DNA must be one of the smallest specimens." (Pp. 82-83.)

One can only imagine the DNA improbability of a human being.

"In a universe only 10^{18} seconds old it is obvious that life could not have evolved by chance." (Foster, p.83.)

Behe defines *irreducible complex* as "a single system composed of several well-matched, interacting parts that contribute to the basic function, wherein the removal of any one of the parts causes the system to effectively cease functioning." (P. 39.) He also explains the specificity and complexity of the blood-clotting sequence and the odds of it happening by chance: "Such an event would not be expected to happen even if the universe's [estimated] ten-billion year life were compressed into a single second and relived every second for ten billion years." (P. 96.)

Such is the impossibility of chance creation in the biological world.

16. The statistics and examples used in "Improbability" were inspired by and taken from Foster's *The Philosophical Scientists*.

17. Steven Weinberg, *Dreams of A Final Theory* (New York: Vintage Books, 1994), p. 6. The final theory is defined by the author as follows: "Think of the space of scientific principles as being filled with arrows, pointing toward each principle and away from the others by which it is explained. These arrows of explanation have already revealed a remarkable pattern: they do not form separate disconnecting clumps, representing independent sciences, and they do not wander aimlessly—rather they are all connected, and if followed backward they all seem to flow from a common starting point. This starting point, to which all explanations may be traced, is what I mean by a final theory."

18. "Mutation": See also notes 6 and 7. I express in my poem "Evolution's Fraud" that all plant life on the earth came about as follows: "As for me, a Husbandman I see/ planting seeds in his nursery." I feel that an omnificent, omniscient, and omnipotent Creator could easily arrange to bring seeds, as well as all living creatures, from other worlds and transplant them here. With intergalactic travel on the horizon, such an event even seems possible

for finite man.

Darwinian evolution is a mathematically improbable theory. It is reckless, cruel, amoral, delusive, and impersonal. It is inadequate in nearly every area in which it is applied. It is certainly inadequate in explaining the overwhelming complexity of molecular biology and life's order, beauty, variety, magnificence, and glory. (See note 11.) It is inadequate in explaining linguistics and information.

It is interesting to note that only humans have the capacity for using complex language, writing, thinking in the abstract, building complex structures, performing complex medical procedures, worshiping, and expressing philosophical views.

The fact that these abilities and traits are absent in the animal world cast serious doubt on the theory of evolution. If evolution were factual there would be evidence, to some marked degree, of these traits in the many "evolving" species.

Darwinian evolution implies mindless chance and life being an accident in time. It implies disintegration, confusion, and oblivion. It implies atheism, nihilism, and death. It implies nothing.

Creation implies a responsible purpose. It implies immortal genes and an ancestral record. It implies a future beyond the visible. It implies consistency and patterns in the cosmos, which is the real message of stasis in the fossil record, and order rather than confusion in all of nature.

I feel that even so-called "directed evolution" is a philosophical theory without empirical evidence and is an attempt to bring creationism in harmony with evolutionary science, which has its basis in materialism. It is an unnecessary theory .

Some proponents of directed evolution postulate that all the species were preprogramed in the beginning, then left alone to do their evolving or mutating. This casts the Creator as distant and uninterested as well as impersonal, and implies disrespect by using other species to arrive at "the image of deity." (Genesis 1:27, *Holy*

Bible, King James translation.)

The theory of directed evolution opens the door to confusion and uncertainty in the cosmos, and carries the nebulous sounds of all evolutionary philosophies—sounds of "it is possible," "at least hypothetically," "it is easy to imagine."

Because of the molecular information available today, proponents of directed evolution like to use this information (as do all evolutionists) to explain how evolution took place or could easily be directed. They hypothesize that since the DNA sequence between many of the species is trivial that the Creator could easily preprogram the different species into the genetic code. Then mutation from one species to another could be accomplished in the DNA sequence space by a process of "functionless intermediates." In other words, the process of mutating intermediaries would take place but remain unexpressed in the functionless part of the DNA sequence space. It would remain unexpressed until called upon by preprogramming to produce a new species. (See Michael Denton, *Nature's Destiny* [New York: The Free Press, 1998], pp. 265-98.)

This reminds us of evolution by saltation (sudden leaps after long periods of stasis), which was invented to explain the reason for the lack of transitional forms in the fossil record. See note 7 for information about the problems facing paleontologists because of the lack of evidence in the fossil record for gradualism.

The question is: Without some kind of gradualism, how did the new species begin from its predecessor species? Did the functionless DNA suddenly activate in, for instance, the sperm and egg of chimpanzees to produce human beings—males from some chimpanzees and females from others—who would then grow up under the tutelage of chimp parents and start the human race?

The example seems as unreasonable as the theory itself.

Even though the DNA sequences are close in many of the different species, the morphological differences are enormous. This would suggest that there are vast, unknown differences hidden away in the genetic code.

Because of the enormous differences in the species it is a stretch of the imagination the think that one species could suddenly make the leap to another species without any trace of intermediaries. And according to science, as indicated in note 7, there is an absence of transitional forms (intermediaries), in the fossil record. This would suggest that there are none.

According to many scientists there is an inescapable conflict in trying to merge evolutionary science with creationism.

I find all evolutionary theories unconvincing and inadequate in their attempt to explain the profuse display, specificity, and order of life.

I feel that all life forms have their likeness elsewhere and represent patterns of consistency throughout time. All nature and the biological wonders familiar to us are not alone in the cosmos.

Microevolution (improvement within the species) is empirical and evident. We see it as we continue to influence improvements within the species. Beyond this the species remain stasis (well defined).

19. Some of the ideas, wordage, and anatomical information in "The Mystery of Life" and other poems related to human anatomy came from the scholarly writings and examples set forth in *The Incredible Machine*.

20. Ralph Waldo Emerson, *Essays* (Franklin Center, Pennsylvania: The Franklin Library, 1981), p. 251.

21. A. Dressy Morrison, *Man Does Not Stand Alone* (New York: Fleming H. Revell Company, no date), p. 59. Ideas and inspiration for "Purpose" came from this source.

22. "Receding Faith" was inspired by Matthew Arnold's poem "Dover Beach." It can be found in *The Classic Hundred Poems*, edited by William Harm (New York: Columbia University Press, 1990), pp. 185-86.

23. Emerson, "The Poet," in *Essays*, p. 245. *Humble wanderer* means that this cosmic message or conviction, "this great calm presence of the creator," comes not to those who have lost the divine nature of their first being by lascivious contagion but that the sublime vision comes to the pure and simple soul. Emerson quotes John Milton as saying that "the epoch poet, he who shall sing with the gods and their descent unto men, must drink water out of a wooden bowl," meaning water unpolluted from the "Devil's wine." The recipient must be a humble, seeking person to experience this epoch symphony.

24. Will Durant, *Story of Philosophy* (New York: Simon and Schuster, 1926), pp. 400-1. The thoughts and some of the wording in this paragraph in the poem "Epilogue" were inspired and taken from the above source.

25. Matthew 18:6, *Holy Bible*, King James translation. "But whoso shall offend one of these little ones which believe in me, it were better for him that a millstone were hanged about his neck, and that he were drowned in the depth of the sea."

26. When amorality's hedonistic rampages rumble through the faithless drought; when humanity tires of the moral and religious restraints that inhibit natural, carnal tendencies, the resulting wanton associations and environment that inevitably follow bring conduct to a state of depraved anarchy. When this occurs, which is inevitable under these conditions, humanity eventually tires of its hedonistic freedom and seeks a more orderly and restrained society. It eventually learns that within the once-derided moral restraints is the only secure place of peace, freedom, and happiness.

The inspiration for the poem "Restraints" came from reading a quote by Ortega Y Gassett in his *Revolt of the Masses* (New York: W.W. Norton, 1957), pp. 135-36. "Decalogues retain from the time they were written on stone or bronze their character of heaviness. . . . Lower ranks the world over are tired of being ordered and commanded, and with holiday air take advantage of a period freed from burdensome imperatives. But the holiday does not last long. Without commandments, obliging us to live after a certain fashion, our existence is that of the 'unemployed.' This is the terrible spiritual situation in which the best youth of the world finds itself today. By dint of feeling itself free, exempt from restrictions, it feels itself empty. . . . Before long there will be heard throughout the planet a formidable cry, rising like the howling of innumerable dogs to the stars, asking for someone or something to take command, to impose an occupation, a duty."

27. Nathaniel Hawthorne, *The Scarlet Letter* (Garden City, New York: International Collectors Library, no date), p. 211.